THE GUNSMITH

458

The Gunsmith Saloon

Books by J.R. Roberts
(Robert J. Randisi)

The Gunsmith series

Lady Gunsmith series

Angel Eyes series

Tracker series

Mountain Jack Pike series

COMING SOON!

The Gunsmith
459 – The Imperial Crown

For more information visit:
www.SpeakingVolumes.us

THE GUNSMITH

458

The Gunsmith Saloon

J.R. Roberts

SPEAKING VOLUMES, LLC
NAPLES, FLORIDA
2020

The Gunsmith Saloon

ISBN 978-1-64540-231-2

Chapter One

"Partners?" Clint Adams asked.

"Full partners," Rick Hartman said.

"You never take partners."

"Well," Rick said, "you'd be a little more than a partner."

"How so?"

"I want to call it the Gunsmith Saloon."

"Get out of here!"

***

Clint had returned from a long trip which had taken him from Denver to Washington, D.C. and then to Florida. Upon his return to Denver, he reacquainted himself with the fulsome Samantha Carlson, managed to have a meal with his friend Talbot Roper, and then headed to Labyrinth, Texas for some R&R.

Labyrinth was Clint's home away from home, only there was no home for him to be away from. This was the only place he ever felt he could relax, if not totally. He still wore his gun, still hung it on the bedpost at night, still answered a knock at his hotel room door with the Colt in his hand. But compared to everywhere else he'd been or would be going, he was relaxed.

Part of that relaxation came compliments of his friend, Rick Hartman. Clint was welcome to eat and drink in Rick's Place for free, he could play poker or faro if he wanted, or just spend time with the girls. Everyone knew he and Rick were friends, and that worked in both their favors.

He was sitting at his friend's regular table after having been in Labyrinth for a week, before Rick brought up the subject of a proposed partnership.

"When did this idea pop into your head?" Clint asked.

"Well, you know I'm always looking for new business ventures," Rick said.

"That's true," Clint said. "For a man who never leaves town, you're spread out pretty far and wide when it comes to business."

"I own lots of places, and have people running them for me," Rick said, "but you're right, I have no partners. But this one . . . this one's got your name all over it, or it will if you agree."

"'The Gunsmith Saloon,'" Clint repeated.

"Has a ring to it, doesn't it?" Rick asked. "It should attract customers."

"And trouble."

"Only if you're there," Rick pointed out.

"So you're saying you want my name, but you don't want me to be there."

"Well," Rick said, "not exactly."

"Then what are you saying," Clint asked, "exactly?"

"I'd like you to go to the location, check it out, and if it's a fit, get it up and running for me. For us."

Clint had a piece of several businesses throughout the West—saloons, mines, even a freight business—all small percentages that kept money flowing into his bank accounts. This would be a fifty-fifty partnership with a proven businessman and would probably keep his accounts healthy for some time.

"Okay, where are we talking about?" Clint asked.

"Laramie, Wyoming."

"Why Laramie?"

"It's near the borders of Colorado and Nebraska, and it's growing. They just opened a University there."

"And what's the location?"

"The old Bucket of Blood," Rick said.

"Wasn't that the place owned by the brothers, Con and Ace Moyer, and their cousin, Steve Long?"

"Yeah," Rick said, "they were half-brothers, and they ran the county. Long was Laramie's first marshal, but that was years ago. They're gone now."

"They were lynched in eighteen sixty-eight," Clint pointed out.

"The town isn't as lawless as it once was. Like I said, it's growing."

"Do you know who the law is there?"

"They have a marshal named July Jackson."

"Colorful name," Clint said, "but I never heard of him."

"I don't know much about him," Rick said.

"What else do you know about Laramie?"

"It's in Albany county, which has a population of over six thousand. There are several large ranches in the area, and some smaller ones. They have a mayor and a town council."

"So I'd have to deal with them."

"At some point, yes," Rick said, "but you'd also have to hire somebody to manage the place for us."

Clint picked up his beer and sipped from it.

"So, whataya say?" Rick asked. "Partners?"

"I'll have to give it some thought," Clint said. "Not so much about being partners with you. That's not a problem. But the name of the place . . ."

"I get it," Rick said. "I expected you to want to think it over. Get back to me in a few days. Meanwhile, finish that beer and I'll freshen you up."

Chapter Two

Melanie Jones was the lady barber in Labyrinth, who Clint had met the last time he was in town. He had gotten a haircut from her, and a lot more. This time when he arrived, he was glad to see she was still there, and still in business.

They got reacquainted pretty quick, and in his hotel room that night, he told her about Rick's offer.

"So, what do you think?" she asked.

"Anything Rick gets involved in usually makes money," he said.

"Yeah, but this is gonna have your name on it," she said. "Maybe you should get sixty percent, and him forty."

"That's not the point," he said. "The point is do I want to be involved, at all. And do I want to go to Laramie to look at the location?"

"Well," she said, rolling over in bed and running her hand over his chest, "I say, not right now."

She was gloriously naked next to him, her full body and smooth, pale skin on display. Her dark hair was long and smelled clean as it tickled his nose while she kissed his neck.

He ran his hand over her back and down to her ass, and she rolled over so that she was lying on top of him, her breasts crushed against his chest, her crotch against his. She kissed him in a hot fervor that he matched, while his now totally hard cock was trapped between them.

She kept rubbing her crotch against his until her pubic patch was good and wet, and then she began rubbing it over the length of him, wetting him, as well.

"If you are gonna leave town to go to Laramie," she said, "then we need to do more of this, so I can be worn out and able to wait for you to come back."

"You're telling me you haven't been with another man since I was here last?"

"I'm saying I haven't been with a man like you since you left," she said. She moved her hips, reached down to hold his cock so she could slide down on it. "Ah. Jesus . . ." she gasped.

She sat up then, so she could start riding him saying, "And if you leave . . . I'm not gonna find another man . . . like you until . . . you come . . . back . . ."

"Well," Clint said, placing his hands on her hips, "we've got at least tonight."

She glared down at him.

"You're leavin' tomorrow?"

"I haven't decided," he said, "but we have all night."

"I'm gonna make the most of it, then," she said.

6

She hopped off him, leaving his hard, wet penis begging for more, shimmied down and immediately took it into her mouth . . .

***

"Oh my God," he said, later. His legs were still shaking from the explosion.

"So you're really thinking about doing this?" she asked.

"It's a possibility," he said, reaching over to run his fingers over her right breast and nipple. "I'm just going to give it a little more thought."

"Tonight?"

"No." He rolled over and kissed her nipple. "No more tonight. Now I'm just going to concentrate on you."

"Well then," she said, spreading her legs, "start concentrating . . ."

***

"Oooooh," she moaned, as they rolled apart, "this is why I don't want you to leave."

"I have to leave, eventually," he told her.

"I know that," she said. "I'm not asking you to stay forever. I'd never do that."

"Okay." He settled down onto his back.

"And we can still talk about the saloon thing, if you want," she said. "I'd like to help you make up your mind."

"You know," he said, "I wouldn't mind owning a successful gambling hall and saloon. I have a piece of a couple of saloons, but a gambling palace . . . that would be something totally different."

"Yes, it would," she said. She was also lying on her back, with her hands folded across her stomach. He tried not to look at her, though, because seeing those breasts, that skin, and her beautiful face, he knew they'd stop talking again.

"So he wants to call it the Gunsmith Saloon?" she asked. "Not the Gunsmith Palace, or something like that?"

"We'd still have to discuss it," he said. "But there's no point naming the place until we're sure we're going to do it."

"And you can't be sure unless you go to Laramie and take a look," she said.

"That's right." He made the mistake of turning his head and looked at her, which made him reach for her. "But let's talk about that tomorrow."

Chapter Three

The next day Clint and Melanie had breakfast together, and then she went to open her shop. He stayed in the café and had some more coffee on his own, thinking about Rick's offer of partnership.

He kept to himself until about midday, when he walked into Rick's Place. The bartender, Shiloh, grinned at him and asked, "Beer?"

"No, not yet," Clint said. "Rick come down?"

"Yep, he's in his office." He pointed to the back of the room.

"Thanks," Clint said.

He walked to the back, knocked on the office door and entered. Rick looked up from the paperwork that was spread over his desk.

"Don't worry about all this," he said to Clint. "You won't have to deal with any of this shit when we're partners."

"Yeah, about that—"

"Don't tell me you decided to say no," Rick said, sitting back in his chair.

"I haven't really decided yet," Clint said.

"What else can I say to convince you?"

"Why don't you go to Laramie yourself and take a look?" Clint asked.

"Even if I did," Rick said, "you'd still have to agree to the name of the place. Before you do that, I thought you'd want a look."

"You're probably right," Clint said.

"And you said yourself, I never leave town," Rick reminded him. "So I need you to do this for me. For us."

Clint fell into silent thought. Rick thought he had him, so he pushed.

"You've got nothing else going, right?"

"Right."

"No other friends asking for help?"

"None."

"No damsels in distress for you to run to?"

"I don't run to damsels—"

"Yeah, you do."

"Okay, yeah, I do, but I have none now."

"Then what's the problem?"

"I just got here," Clint said, "and I'm having a good time with Melanie."

"Ah," Rick said, "our lovely barber. You know, I'm letting her cut my hair now."

"As long as that's all that's going on," Clint said.

"You getting possessive about a woman now?" Rick asked. "Maybe you do need a distraction."

"You might be right about that," Clint said.

Clint had met two women recently that he found him-self thinking a lot about: Samantha in Denver and Mela-nie in Labyrinth.

"So you'll do it?"

"Yeah," Clint said, "yeah, I'll do it."

"That's great!" Rick said. "Look, I'll give you some money for the trip, for your expenses."

"I'll take it," Clint said.

"I can get it back when we start showing a profit from the Gunsmith Saloon."

"That's the Rick Hartman, businessman that I know," Clint said.

"Let's go out and have a drink to our new partner-ship," Rick said.

"Hey, I agreed to go to Laramie and have a look at the setup, but I haven't agreed to a partnership, just yet."

"Let's go have a drink, anyway." Rick stood up. "Come on."

***

"So you're going," Melanie said, that night.

"Yep," Clint said.

"When?"

"Tomorrow."

11

"But once you've had a look, you'll have to come back and talk with Rick, right?"

"Right."

"So you won't be gone so long, this time."

"I doubt it. I'm just going there to take a look and report back to Rick."

"Is he going to want you to make the buy?" Melanie asked.

"If I agree to be partners, probably."

She folded her arms across her large breasts, hiding those glorious nipples from view.

"That means you'll have to set it up and hire somebody to manage it."

"It doesn't matter," Clint said, gliding a hand across her bare belly. "I'll be back. And when I do get back . . ." He lowered his voice.

"Yes?" she sighed.

"I'll need a haircut."

Chapter Four

Clint had not been to Laramie in quite some time. And when he was there, he had not taken a good look at The Bucket of Blood. This time around, it would be a priority.

He rode in as quietly and unassuming as he could, wanting to keep a low profile, at least in the beginning. According to Rick, The Bucket of Blood had long been off limits to anyone who might want to purchase it, but had now been put up for sale by the bank.

Often, upon arriving in a town, he would ask someone where the closest livery was. On this day, however, he simply kept riding until he came to one, not wanting to call any attention to himself. Of course, simply riding into town on Eclipse, his Darley Arabian, was bound to attract *some* notice.

Once inside the livery, though, he did ask the hostler for advice about which hotel to stay in. The man—in his sixties and obviously very experienced at his job—was beside himself at the thought of having a horse like Eclipse in his stable.

"I'd say the Laramie Valley Inn," the man said. "They'll treatcha real good there."

"Thanks," Clint said. "I'll take a look."

"It's right down the street," the hostler said. "You would've come to it if you kept ridin' past here—which I'm sure glad you didn't."

"What's your name?"

"Hagan."

"Is that your first, or last name?"

"It's my name," Hagan said. "It's what folks call me."

"All right, Hagan . . . take good care of my horse."

"Mister, you can bet I will."

Clint grabbed his saddlebags and rifle and left the livery.

***

The Laramie Valley Inn was a two story hotel that looked like an old building that had recently been renovated. There were a half dozen chairs set up on the porch, with several men seated in them. They cast curious looks at Clint as he entered the lobby, but, after he passed, they went back to what they were doing.

At the desk, he signed the register and the clerk asked him how long he thought he would be staying.

"Probably several days," he answered. "I have some business in town."

"I could give you a room overlooking the front of the hotel, sir," the clerk offered.

"I'd prefer something away from the front, thanks." Clint said.

"Of course." The clerk handed him a key. "Room five, sir. It overlooks the alley."

"Thank you."

The room was clean and well-appointed, with no access from the one window. He dropped his rifle and saddlebags onto the bed, which had a very firm mattress.

It was too late in the day to go to the bank to talk about The Bucket of Blood, but he could walk over and have a look at the outside. He could also stop at the marshal's office and let him know he was in town.

He left the room and went back down to the lobby. On the porch there were still two men sitting in chairs, about six feet apart. They each seemed to be alone with their thoughts, minding their own business. Clint did the same and kept on walking.

He decided to see the marshal before taking a look at the saloon.

***

He found the marshal's office on his own, rather than asking anyone. It was in a prominent position on East Ivinson Street, which seemed to be a major thoroughfare for Laramie.

As he entered the office, he found himself in a large room which had the gun racks and desk found in most sheriff's and marshal's offices, but much more space to move around. In fact, the desk was a good distance from the door. Against the back wall was a doorway which obviously would lead to the cell block.

The man seated at the desk was in his late forties, with steel-grey hair and a solid chin. On wall pegs behind him were hung his hat and gun belt.

"Marshal Jackson?" Clint asked.

"That's right," the man said in a deep, gravelly voice. "Can I help you?"

"My name is Clint Adams. I just rode into town."

Jackson sat back in his chair.

"Lookin' for trouble?"

"No, sir," Clint said. "I'm here on business."

"Gunsmith business?"

"In a way," Clint said. "A friend of mine is thinking of buying The Bucket of Blood. He asked me to stop here and have a look at it, so I can advise him on whether or not to do it."

"He wants to reopen The Bucket of Blood?" Jackson asked.

"Under a different name."

"I don't know how people in town will feel about that," the lawman said.

"That's something else I can find out, while I'm here."

"Well, it's just up the street," Jackson said. "But you'll need someone from the bank to let you in."

"I'll take care of that part tomorrow," Clint said. "Today I'll just look at the outside."

"So then, you're not here lookin' for anyone," Marshal Jackson said.

"No, sir," Clint said. "Just what I said."

"Can you stay out of trouble?"

"I can try."

"Well," Jackson said, "I guess that's all I can ask. Thanks for comin' in and lettin' me know."

"Sure thing." Clint turned to leave, then stopped. "One more thing."

"Yeah?"

"Is your name really July Jackson?" Clint asked.

Jackson stared at him for a few moments, then sat forward in his chair.

"My sisters' names are May and June," he said. "What do you think?"

"Very nice names," Clint said, and left.

17

Chapter Five

Clint walked up the street and found The Bucket of Blood only two blocks from the marshal's office. It took up the better part of one side of the block. It had a large front door with an overhang bearing the faded words THE BUCKET OF BLOOD that could easily be painted over.

There were windows on either side of the door, and a second floor with windows overlooking the street. At the moment, however, all the glass was gone, and they were boarded up.

There was a street on one side and an alley on the other. He walked down the alley, saw more boarded up windows, and then got to the back, where there was a lot of room for buckboards making deliveries, pulling in from the side street to the back door.

He walked back around to the front, crossed the street and stared at the place.

Suddenly a door opened behind him and a woman said, "Oh no."

He turned, saw an attractive-if-slightly-faded woman standing in the open door of a store. A glance at the window showed women's clothing and hats.

"Can I help you?" he asked.

"Don't tell me you're thinkin' about reopenin' that place," she said, pointing.

"I might," he said, "but not as The Bucket of Blood. Why?"

"My mother had this shop back during those days," she said, "and drunks were always breaking these windows every night."

"That wouldn't happen again," he said. "I can assure you of that."

"Oh, really?" She stepped out of the store to stand next to him, her arms folded across her chest. She was tall, svelte, in good physical condition. He thought maybe away from her job and dressed up she would attract a lot of looks. "You can guarantee that?"

"Pretty much."

"You're gonna be the owner?"

"One of them," he said.

"And there won't be any drunken cowboys in there?"

"Well," Clint said, "yes, I mean, it will be a saloon, after all—"

"Ah-ha!" she said.

"Look," Clint said, "I'm not even sure we're going to buy it. I'm here to take a look."

"Did you just get to town?"

"A few hours ago."

"Laramie's a good place to live," she said, "but we don't need the Wild West to come callin'."

"I understand . . . Miss?"

"Mrs. Wells," she said, "Abby Wells."

"Mrs. Wells," he said. "if you're afraid that your husband will start—"

"I'm a widow," she said. "My husband died years ago. Look, I'm just askin' you to let me know if you're gonna reopen. Then maybe I'll have to make some decisions."

"Like what?"

"Like movin' my shop."

"This is a good location on a main street," he said.

"I know it," she said. "But if there's a saloon across the street . . ."

"Saloon, gambling hall and theater."

"Theater?"

"With a stage."

"That does sound classier than what The Bucket of Blood used to be," she said. "What's your name?"

"I'm Clint," he said, putting out his hand. "Glad to meet you, Mrs. Wells."

"You can call me Abby," she said, shaking his hand. "That is, until I find out you're a liar."

"Deal," he said.

Chapter Six

The next morning Clint decided on breakfast, and then a visit to the bank. The only thing was, he didn't know which bank. There were apparently three in Laramie.

He had seen a café down the street from his hotel that advertised, out front, that they served breakfast and lunch. He decided to try it and save the dining room in his hotel for supper.

After a good breakfast of steak-and-eggs, he walked around town, looking for the three banks, trying to decide which one to try first. Then he got an idea and walked back to The Bucket of Blood. He took a closer look at the front door and found a notice with the name of the bank that held the mortgage on the building: Laramie First Depositor's Bank.

He walked directly to the bank, entered and saw three teller windows ahead of him, and two desks off to the left. He could also see the safe, and a door with the words BANK MANAGER on it.

"Hello, sir," a woman's voice said.

She had risen from her desk and walked over to him. She was young, in her twenties, pretty with very bright, blue eyes and auburn hair.

"Can we help you?" she asked. "You're not a regular depositor?"

"No, I'm not," he said. "I just got to town yesterday."

"Well, welcome to Laramie," she said. "What can we do for you?"

"I'm interested in seeing the old Bucket of Blood property."

"Oh," she said, with a smile, "well, you're in luck, then. I happen to be just the person to see about that. Would you come to my desk?"

"Thank you."

When they reached the desk, she sat, invited him to sit in the chair next to her. There was a nameplate on the desk that said MISS RAYLAND.

"Do you know much about the property?" she asked, opening her drawer and removing a file.

"Not very much," he said. "I know who used to own it, and I know it's been closed up for some time."

"Yes, indeed," she said. "We've only been showing it since our new mayor came into office. He happens to be the last of the family who owned and ran the place."

"What was his relation to them?"

"His name is Mayor Avner Long. Con and Ace Moyer were his uncles, as well as Steve Long. So he's the only family member left, and he owns it. He's given us the right to negotiate with any would-be buyers."

"Oh, I see," Clint said.

"The family never wanted to sell it," she went on, "but when he became mayor, he talked to Mr. Edward, our bank manager, and agreed to allow the bank to take care of the sale."

"So," Clint asked, "when can I see it?"

"Don't you want to know what the selling price is?" she asked.

"I'd like to see it, first."

"Oh, well, right," she said, "but in that case, I'll need your name."

"It's Clint Adams."

She started to write and then stopped and looked at him. He could see the recognition in her eyes. He'd seen it many times before.

"*The* Clint Adams?" she asked.

"The only one I know," he said.

"Wow," she said, and finished writing. "Let me just tell my boss I'm going, and we'll walk over there." She also opened her top desk drawer and took out a set of keys.

***

When they reached the front of the building, she slipped a key into the front door lock and opened it.

Inside, the two batwing doors were each hanging from one hinge.

They walked in carefully, so as not to knock them off.

"Well," she said, "here it is."

He walked further into the large interior to look around. There was a long bar, a wide stage, broken tables and chairs, a lopsided piano. The ceilings were very high, and there was still some crystal in the chandeliers. From the second floor you could look down over a railing—or could've, if the railing was still there.

"There's an office in the back," Miss Rayland said, "eight rooms upstairs. Also, in the back is a large room for private poker games and a storeroom."

"Is there a kitchen?" Clint asked.

"There is, just behind the bar."

Clint walked around behind the bar, where there were still shards of broken bottles on the floor. Miss Rayland waited in the main room while he entered the kitchen, looked at the stove and the oven, and a three-legged table with no chairs.

He came back out and leaned on the bar. In his mind's eye, he could see what Rick Hartman would do with this place. He knew his friend could draw up some plans in Texas, plans that would be followed by a Laramie crew. It could be something he wanted to be part of. The thing he still wasn't sure of was whether or not he wanted to put his name on it.

"What do you think?" Miss Rayland asked.

"It's very impressive," Clint said, "that is, it could be." He looked at her. "I met a woman who has a store right across the street. She said she didn't want this place to be reopened. At least, not as a saloon."

"That must be Abby," Miss Rayland said.

"Exactly," Clint said. "Are there any other people in town who are against the place reopening?"

"Oh, I'm sure there are," she said. "You'll have to deal with the mayor and the town council."

"I expected that."

She glanced around, then looked at him.

"Would this be sufficient for what you and your partners have in mind?" she asked.

"I'm sure it would," he said.

He didn't bother explaining to her that the problem was him, not Rick.

"Then shall we go back to the bank and talk price?" she asked.

"Why not?"

Chapter Seven

Back at the bank, they sat at Miss Rayland's desk and discussed the price.

"I'll have to send a telegram to my partner about this," Clint said, finally. "Plus, I'll have to figure out how much it's going to cost us to get the place back into shape."

"Will you be using local workers, Mr. Adams?" she asked. "I can steer you to some good men."

"That'd be great," Clint said. "By the way, do I have to keep calling you Miss Rayland?"

"No, of course not," she said. "My first name is Constance, but everyone calls me Connie."

"Connie," he said. "That's good. I'm Clint."

"Clint, we just need to do one more thing."

"What's that?"

"Have you meet the bank manager, Mr. Edward. Do you mind waiting while I see if he's available?"

"No problem."

"Thank you."

She got up from behind her desk, walked to the manager's door, knocked and entered. Clint noticed that the two male tellers on duty watched every step she took.

After about ten minutes, she came back out and waved to Clint. He stood and walked over to her.

"Mr. Edward would like to meet you," she said.

"Lead the way."

"He'd like to talk to you alone." She held the door open for him.

"Thank you."

He entered the office, saw a small man who was made even smaller by the huge desk. Clint noticed he was wearing pince-nez glasses.

"Mr. Adams?" the man said, remaining behind his desk. "Please, have a seat."

"Mr. Edward," Clint said. "Glad to meet you." He sat across from the man, who removed the glasses from his nose and allowed them to hang from a black ribbon.

"I understand you're interested in purchasing The Bucket of Blood property."

"The former Bucket of Blood, yes," Clint said. "I'm interested."

"But you and Miss Rayland haven't come to an agreement on a price yet?"

"No, not yet."

"According to her, you have a partner you'll need to confer with."

"Yes," Clint said, "I'll be sending him a telegram."

"And is he the money man?"

"He is."

"I see. Well, we are rather anxious to get it up and running again. It's always been rather a legend around here."

"I don't think you understand," Clint said. "We won't be reopening The Bucket of Blood. It'll have a new name."

"Oh," Edward said, sitting back. "Oh, I see."

"Is that a problem?"

"Well," Edward said, "to be truthful, I'd have to talk with the mayor."

"So it's a problem if I want to buy it and change the name? It's been closed a long time."

"Just let me talk to the mayor," Edward said. "Meanwhile, you work on the price with Miss Rayland, and contact your partner."

"Okay," Clint said. "But you let me know if I have to talk to the mayor to make this deal."

"I will," Edward said. "I think he might quite like the idea of having the Gunsmith go into business in Laramie."

"You know," Clint said, "that doesn't mean I'll be here all the time."

"But sometimes," the bank manager said.

"Sure," Clint said. "Sometimes."

"Thank you for coming in to see me, sir," Edward said, putting those weird glasses back on his nose. "Miss Rayland is at your disposal."

Clint stood up and left the manager's office. Miss Rayland smiled at him from her desk as he walked over.

"All set?" she asked.

"Not exactly," he replied.

"Problems?"

"You didn't tell the manager that we wouldn't be reopening The Bucket of Blood."

"Oh," she said, "I knew he'd want to talk with you about that."

"Uh-huh," Clint said, "and the mayor?"

"Yes," she said, "he might want it to be called The Bucket of Blood, but I'm sure Mr. Edward can talk to him. You see, he really wants to get it sold."

"Are there any other buyers?"

"Not at this time," she said.

"All right, then," he said, "why don't we talk money?"

She put her hand on her chin and asked, "Why don't we do that at supper?"

Chapter Eight

Clint got as many facts as he could into a short telegram to Rick. In his opinion the place was a good buy, but needed work.

While he was at the telegraph office, Connie Rayland had time to get changed for supper. She chose the restaurant in Clint's hotel, which was a sign for him that the place was good. He'd had a small supper there the night before, but needed something more elaborate to judge it by.

When he got to the hotel, Connie wasn't in the lobby or the restaurant. He went back out to the porch to sit and wait for her.

A woman stepped up onto the porch. At first he didn't recognize her. At the bank she had been dressed for work, wearing a business suit and a severe hair style. Now, she was in a blue dress, with her hair worn flowing loose. It made her seem older, more sophisticated.

"Connie," he said, standing. "I didn't recognize you."

"I have to dress differently for the bank," she explained. "Are you hungry?"

"Very."

"They have a wonderful osso buco here."

He didn't know what that was, but if she was recommending it, he was ready to try it.

The Laramie Valley Inn Restaurant had a maître d' who showed them to a table in the crowded dining room.

"I'm underdressed," he said, as they sat. "Sorry."

"You look fine," she said.

But he had attracted attention, walking across the dining room wearing a gun. Or perhaps it had been Connie who had attracted the attention.

A waiter came and presented them with menus, took their orders of a glass of wine for her and a beer for him.

He found the osso buco she had mentioned on the menu. It was a braised veal shank prepared in an Italian sauce.

When the waiter came, they ordered two.

"So," she said, "did you send your telegram?"

"I did."

"Any response?"

"Not yet," he answered. "I expect to find something waiting at the desk for me when we're done here."

"That would be nice."

"Did you hear anything from your boss?"

"I did," she said. "After you left, he told me not to make a firm deal until I heard from him."

"So I assume that means, after he talks to the mayor."

"I'm sure."

31

"I should know by tomorrow whether or not I want to make an offer," Clint said.

"So should I," she said.

The waiter came with their suppers.

"For now," she said, "let's just eat."

"Agreed."

***

Clint found the osso buco delicious. The veal shank was so tender it fell off the bone.

"What did you think?" she asked, when they were finished.

"It was great," he said. "I don't think I've ever had anything like it before."

"Good," she said. "Now for dessert."

"Something else new?" he asked.

"Unless you just like good pie," she said.

"I love good pie," he said, "especially peach."

"Let's see if they have it."

The waiter said they did. He brought Clint a slice of peach, Connie apple, and both of them coffee. Both the pie and the coffee were a match for the osso buco.

"This might've been the best meal I've had in a while," he said, when they were done.

"I agree," she said. "I've always wondered how it would be."

That surprised Clint.

"I thought you'd been here before," he said.

"Just the opposite," she said. "I wanted to come because I'd only heard about it from some of our larger depositors."

"Well then, I'm glad we came," he said.

They walked out to the lobby together.

"Can I walk you home?" he asked. "Or get you a ride?"

"Neither," she said. "I told you, I've never been here before."

"And?"

"And I'd like to see one of the rooms," she said, with a smile.

"*My* room?" he asked.

"That *is* the only one you have a key for, isn't it?" she asked.

"Well, yes—"

"This way?" she asked, pointing.

"Yes," he said, "that way."

She linked her arm in his.

Chapter Nine

Clint wondered if he was reading Connie's intentions correctly.

After checking at the front desk for a telegram and finding nothing, they went upstairs. When they got to his room, he unlocked the door and allowed her to go in first. He didn't think he'd been in Laramie long enough to attract someone who'd try to bushwhack him in his room.

"This is very nice," she said, turning to face him as he closed the door. "But it's not the honeymoon suite, is it?"

"No," Clint said. "It's just an ordinary room."

"The bed looks nice," she said.

"It's very firm."

She sat on it, rubbed it with both hands.

"Show me," she said.

"What?"

"Our business is done for tonight, right?"

"I suppose it is," he agreed.

"Then show me," she said, "how firm your mattress is."

To confirm what her intentions were, she lifted one foot, and then the other, to remove her shoes. Then she stood and slipped her dress off, tossed it aside, and got back on the bed, still wearing her chemise.

"Is this all right?" she asked, lying back on the bed. "Or am I being too forward."

"Not too forward," he said, "but it's a surprise. I mean, you work in a bank."

"And that makes me a certain kind of girl?"

"I thought it did," Clint said. "I thought you were quiet, shy, smart—"

"I am smart," she said, cutting him off. "But shy and quiet, not so much."

"I can see that now."

"Well," she invited, sitting up, "come over here and see it." She pulled her chemise up over her head, tossed it away, and then once again reclined, this time totally naked. She had a lovely body, with small breasts and sleek legs.

He walked to the bed and, while she watched, unstrapped his gun and hung it on the bedpost.

"I'm assuming that's not for me," she said.

"No," he said, unbuttoning his shirt, "just for safety."

He got his clothes off, and Connie was obviously pleased by what she saw between his legs. She quickly got off the bed on the opposite side, and together they turned the bed down, and then got back on.

"It does seem firm," she said, sliding her hand down between his legs.

"It's a very firm mattress."

She closed her hand around his hard cock and said, "I wasn't talking about the mattress."

***

Rick Hartman read Clint Adams' telegram again.

He trusted Clint's judgment, and was hoping he'd like what he saw in Laramie so much that he would come onboard as a full partner. The price he had suggested in the telegram was more than Rick wanted to spend, but he felt the need to leave the decision in Clint's hands.

He intended to send a telegram to Laramie first thing in the morning.

***

The bank manager, Mr. Edward, waited til the end of the day, and then instead of going to the mayor's office to consult with him, he went to the man's house, one of the largest in Laramie.

Mayor Long was young for a politician, in his forties, a man with quick darting eyes and an even quicker, caustic manner. He took Edward to his den, where he poured a glass of sherry for each of them, and then sat to listen to what the manager had to say.

"So he doesn't want to keep the name Bucket of Blood?" he asked, when Edward was done.

"No, sir," Edward said.

"What name would he put on it?"

"He didn't say," Edward said.

"Or you didn't ask," the mayor pointed out.

"Well, no, but maybe Miss Rayland did."

"Find out in the morning," Long said.

"And if he makes a firm offer?" Edward asked.

"Why don't we see how much he's willing to pay to change the name?" Long suggested.

***

While he might have, at one time, thought her shy and quiet, it took only moments to discover she was energetic and loud during sex.

At one point, while they were kissing, as he slid his hand down between her legs and moved his fingers, her eyes went wide. She groaned very loudly. He thought she was going to scream, but she managed to bite it back.

And if she reacted that way just from his fingers touching her pussy, what would she do when he tasted her with his tongue? He found out just moments later when he bent to the task of licking up her hot, sweet stickiness. She screamed before she was able to once again bite back the sound, and he wondered, just for a moment, if anyone would come pounding at the door to find out what was happening?

No one did . . .

***

Later she showed him that shyness was certainly not part of her make-up, as she avidly sucked his hard cock until he exploded into her mouth. He would have expected that from a prostitute, or even a saloon girl, but not from a bank employee. And she performed the act with skill.

While they were each trying to catch their breath she said, "I've shocked you."

"Not shocked," he said. "Surprised, yes, and in a very good way."

"I know what people think of you when you work in a bank," she said. "I suppose I purposely try to cast off that impression in my private life."

"You've successfully done it, I'd say. In spades!"

"As long as this won't affect our business association," she commented.

"Oh, I think I'll be able to keep one separate from the other," he promised.

"Good," she said, reaching for him, "then maybe we can continue one while we put the other off until tomorrow . . ."

Chapter Ten

Connie rose first, dressed and left, saying she had to go home, bathe and change for work.

"I'll see you at the bank," she said, kissing him good-bye. "And remember . . ."

". . . mum's the word," he finished for her. "Business only."

She smiled and left. And she had gone so early that he was able to roll over and go back to sleep, wrapped in sheets that smelled pleasantly of her . . .

***

Now that the hotel dining room had so impressed him, he decided to have breakfast there. He found Eggs Benedict on their breakfast menu.

"Our cook likes to try different things," the waiter explained. "That's why the osso buco was on our supper menu."

"Well, I'll try the Eggs Benedict, then. And plenty of coffee."

"Yessir."

When the dish came, Clint was impressed with the amount of bacon that was included, and the sauce which the waiter said was "hollandaise."

"It is said this dish originated in Delmonico's in New York City," he told Clint. "Others say is comes from France."

"Well, wherever it comes from," Clint said, around the first bite, "tell the cook it's real good." He sipped the coffee. "All of it."

"I'll tell 'im, sir," the waiter said.

Clint ate his Eggs Benedict with gusto, washing it down with a whole pot of good strong coffee.

***

When he got to the bank, it was open and doing business with several people standing at the teller's cages. He looked over at Connie's desk and saw that it was empty.

"Can I help you, sir?" an older woman asked. She had walked over from another desk.

"Yes, I was supposed to meet with Miss Rayland this morning," he said. "Can you tell me when she'll be in?"

"She should have been in by now," the woman said. "Frankly, I'm worried. She's never late."

"Has anyone checked her home?"

41

"I don't know, sir," she said. "You'd have to talk with Mr. Edward."

"Would you ask him if I can do that?"

"Yes, sir," she said. "Please wait here."

She went to the manager's office, entered, and returned in moments.

"Mr. Edward will see you."

"Thanks."

Clint went to the door and entered.

"Mr. Adams, good-morning," Edward said, from behind his desk. "Have a seat."

"I'll stand, thanks," Clint said. "I understand Connie—Miss Rayland is late."

"Yes," Edward said, "it's never happened before."

"Have you sent anyone to her home to check on her?"

"Not yet," Edward said. "I was giving her more time to get here."

"Well, if you'll tell me where she lives—"

"Why don't you and I continue the negotiations for The Bucket of Blood, while we wait?" Edward interrupted. "I've talked with the mayor. He's not happy about the name change, but he's in favor of the sale."

"That's good," Clint said, "but I'd prefer to keep dealing with one person. Now where does she live?"

Chapter Eleven

Clint followed the directions he was given by the bank manager and found his way to Connie Rayland's house. It was in a section of town that had many other similar houses surrounding it. He was surprised that a young woman could afford her own house, but it possibly had been her parents at one point, or a husband's.

He knocked on the door several times, and when there was no answer, he walked around the house and peered in the windows. The interior looked neat and clean. There was no sign of a struggle that he could see, but he decided to get inside. She might have fallen and been in need of help.

He found a back door which obviously led to the kitchen. Using his shoulder, he forced the door open without damaging it. He'd have to recommend to her that she improve her locks.

Once he was in the kitchen he called out, "Connie!" so as not to frighten her. She could have been feeling sick and was in her bed.

He walked through the first floor of the house, calling another couple of times, then went up the stairs. There were two bedrooms, both empty. He found one that seemed to be hers. It looked unslept in, as if she had never made it home the night before. He was kicking himself for not walking her home.

According to the bank manager, Edward, she had no family in town. Her parents had died. He hadn't asked about a husband, but he went back to the bank to do that. Or it might have been an ex-husband who kept her from getting home . . .

***

"There is no ex-husband," Mr. Edward said. "She's never been married."

"And did her parents leave her that house?"

"No," Edward said, "she bought it last year when I gave her a promotion and a pay raise."

"I see."

"She wasn't there?"

"No, and there was no indication that she ever came home last night."

"W-what should we do?" Edward asked.

"I'm going to talk to Marshal Jackson."

"July's a good man."

"Is he?"

"Well . . . yes," Edward said. "I think so."

"I'll keep that in mind."

"About the purchase—"

"Let's put that off until we find Miss Rayland," Clint suggested. "Or, at least until we discover what happened."

"Whatever you say," the bank manager agreed.

"I'll check back in with you after I talk to the marshal," Clint said, leaving the office.

***

Clint found Marshal July Jackson sitting in his office, as if he had never left since their first meeting.

"Mr. Adams," Jackson said, leaning back in his chair. "What can I do for you today?"

"Do you know a girl named Constance Rayland?"

Johnson frowned.

"Sounds familiar. Gimme more."

"She works at First Depositor's."

"The bank lady," Jackson said. "Kinda meek lookin', but pretty, right?"

Clint nodded.

"What about her?"

"She's missing."

"Whataya mean, missing?"

"I was talking with her yesterday about buying The Bucket of Blood," Clint said. "We were supposed to meet at the bank today, but she's not there. And she's not home. It looks like she didn't get home last night, after we had supper."

"You talk to her boss, Edward?"

"Yes, he hasn't heard from her."

"Well, she's a young woman. She doesn't have to go home if she doesn't want to."

"She's never been late for work before, Marshal," Clint said. "Now she's just not there. Don't you find that suspicious?"

"Did you go to her home?"

"I did. I told you, she's not there."

"Well," Jackson said, "what else do you think I can do? She got family?"

"No."

"And you've been to the bank and to her home?" The lawman shrugged.

"Aren't you going to at least investigate?"

"Look Adams," Jackson said. "I'm a town marshal, not a detective. I jail drunks, shoot dogs, enforce the law, but investigatin' a missin' person? I ain't a Pinkerton."

"Well then, you won't mind if I keep looking around and asking questions," Clint said. "I've actually worked with the Pinkertons a time or two."

Jackson spread his hands.

"Be my guest."

Clint nodded his thanks and left.

Chapter Twelve

Clint was satisfied that he had notified the marshal of his intentions. Now he would concentrate on finding Connie Rayland. He went back to the bank to tell the manager, Mr. Edward, what had happened.

"Still think July Jackson is a good man?" he asked the manager.

"I thought so," Edward said. "This may just be beyond the scope of his abilities." He shrugged. "Maybe she'll turn up on her own."

"Maybe, but I'll keep looking until that happens," Clint said.

"And what about the purchase of The Bucket of Blood?" Edward asked.

"Like I told you before, let's put that aside, for now," Clint said.

"The mayor is quite anxious—"

"Maybe I should talk to him, then," Clint said. "Can you set that up?"

"I can," Edward said. "I'll go and see him now."

"I'll check back with you later," Clint said.

"Hopefully," Edward said, "she'll have turned up by then."

***

Clint spoke with the other bank employees, none of whom were particularly friendly with Connie.

"I asked her to supper a few times," a young male teller said. "I finally gave up."

"She was friendly enough at work, but not outside the bank," the older female clerk said.

When Clint left the bank, he knew nothing more about Connie Rayland. He decided to go to his hotel, since she had left before he did. Perhaps someone there had seen something.

"Sorry, sir," the clerk said. "I didn't see the young lady leave."

"Or maybe you just don't want to embarrass her," Clint suggested. "You should know that she's missing. I'm trying to find her and help if she's in trouble."

The young clerk bit his lip and gave the information some thought.

"All right," he said. "I did see her leave. She went out the front door and was stopped right there by . . . by a man."

"Just one man?" Clint asked. "You don't know his name?"

The clerk bit his lip again.

"Don't worry," Clint said. "You didn't tell me any of this."

"His name is Holden."

"First or last name?"

"Ben Holden."

"Who is he?"

"A gun for hire, usually," the clerk said. "When he's not workin' for anybody, he's just a bully."

"And what happened when they met out front?" Clint asked.

"He grabbed her arm. I could tell he was hurting her. Then he pulled her away from the door and I couldn't see them anymore."

"Can you tell me where to find Holden?"

"I don't know," the clerk said. "I suppose people who hire him find him . . . maybe in a saloon?"

"All right," Clint said. "Thanks."

"Be careful, Mister," the clerk said. "Holden's a hard man."

"Can you tell me someone in town he's worked for?" Clint asked.

"That I don't know," the clerk said. "When he kills somebody, it's usually in a fair fight so the marshal can't do anythin' about it."

"Has the marshal tried?"

"To tell you the truth," the clerk said, "I think the marshal's afraid of him."

"All right," Clint said. "Thanks, again."

Clint started away from the desk, then stopped and turned back.

"One more thing."

"Yes?"

"Do you know if any guests were sitting on the porch when Holden grabbed the lady?"

The clerk thought a moment, then said, "I think Mr. and Mrs. Erickson came in after that happened. They might have been sitting out there and seen it. They're in room nine, down the hall from you."

"Thanks."

As Clint started for the stairs, the clerk said, "They ain't in, right now."

"I'll catch up with them later, then," Clint said, and left the lobby.

Outside on the porch, two men were sitting separately, one smoking and watching the street, the other whittling. Neither paid any attention to him.

He hadn't made the acquaintance with anyone in Laramie except the bank manager, Connie, and Marshal Jackson. He was considering asking the marshal where to find Ben Holden when he saw the manager, Edward, come up onto the porch.

"The mayor will see you now," the man said. "I'll take you over."

They stepped off the porch together.

Chapter Thirteen

"Mr. Mayor," Edward said, as they entered the man's house, "this is Clint Adams. Mr. Adams, Mayor Avner Long."

"Thanks, Henry," the mayor said. "You can go."

This was the first time Clint heard that Edward's given name was Henry. The man nodded and left.

The mayor's house was in a totally different neighborhood than Connie Rayland's, and hers could have easily fit in his living room.

"Please, sit and have a drink," the mayor said, waving to his over-stuffed furniture.

"I'm fine," Clint said. "I don't need anything."

"Henry tells me we have a problem that's holding up the purchase of The Bucket of Blood."

Clint studied the man. He was tall and slender, in his forties, wearing a dark suit he had obviously worn to his office earlier.

"Yes, Miss Rayland, who I was negotiating with, is missing."

"Shouldn't that be his concern, not yours?"

"It so happens I liked the young woman," Clint replied. "I'd like to be sure she's safe."

"I see."

Clint had not only refused the drink but had remained standing. The mayor, also standing, had gotten himself a glass of sherry, and now sat.

"So you're holding up the sale until she can be found?" the mayor asked.

"Until I find her."

"Why you?"

"Because nobody else is looking."

"What if I ordered the marshal to look while you went ahead with your negotiations?"

"I don't think so."

"Why not?"

"He's not qualified."

"And you are?" the mayor asked.

"Yes."

"I guess I wasn't aware of that part of your reputation," the mayor said.

"You can't believe everything you hear," Clint said, "and you can't hear everything."

"Too true," Long said. "Well, I suppose we'll just have to wait for you to find the girl, then. Unless, of course, another buyer comes along."

"After all these years, two in one week would be quite a coincidence," Clint observed, still standing. "Thanks for seeing me, Mr. Mayor."

"My pleasure," Long said, also standing, setting his drink aside. "Let me show you out."

He took Clint to the front door and opened it.

"I hope we can wrap all of this up fairly soon," he said. "The town is rather anxious to see that place up and running, again."

"That's funny," Clint said, "I've spoken to a few citizens who are dead set against it." He said, that even though he had only heard it from the lady across the street from the saloon.

"There are always a few," Mayor Long said. "In the long run it'll be good for the town."

"I'm not thinking about that now," Clint admitted. "I'm just trying to find Miss Rayland."

"I wish you luck, then."

Clint started to leave, then stopped short and said, "One last question, Mayor."

"What's that?"

"Do you know Ben Holden?"

"I know of him," Long said. "I can't say I've ever dealt with the man. Why?"

"Seems he might know where Miss Rayland is. You wouldn't happen to know where I could find him, would you?"

"I'm sorry, no."

Clint nodded and left the mayor's house.

***

He felt he had no choice now but to go to Marshal Jackson. Hopefully, he knew where to find Ben Holden.

"What do you want with Holden?" Jackson asked.

"Apparently, he was seen with Miss Rayland."

"Adams," the marshal said, "Holden is a hard man. If you brace him, push is gonna come to shove."

"I told you before, Marshal, I'm not looking for trouble. But if it finds me, that's another matter."

"Well, if you're lookin' for Ben Holden I can tell you, you're gonna find it."

"Fine, then you do it."

"What?"

"You find him and ask about Constance Rayland."

"Why would I do that?"

"Because you don't want me to do it."

"Hey," Jackson said, "I'm just givin' you a friendly warnin'. That's all."

It occurred to Clint that he had never seen Jackson out from behind his desk. Idly, he wondered how tall the man was?

"Thanks for the warning," he said. "I'll keep it in mind. Now, do you have any idea where I might find him?"

"Try a saloon," Jackson said, "Any saloon."

Clint nodded and left.

Chapter Fourteen

Clint tried six saloons. All six bartenders knew who Ben Holden was. In four of them he was told that Holden had drank there a time or two, but did not make a habit of it. The other two places called Holden a "regular."

The first was The Union House Saloon. The bartender's name was Rex. He looked like an ex-wrestler and was another person who warned Clint about Holden.

"I don't know who you are or why you're lookin' for him, but findin' him can get you dead real fast."

"I understand. When does he usually come in?"

"At night."

"Never in the daytime?" Clint asked.

"I've never seen him in here before dark."

"Does he have friends he drinks with?"

"Friends?" Rex asked. "Holden? No. He drinks alone."

"At the bar, or a table?"

"Table," Rex said. "Once in a while he'll have a girl sit with him."

"Any girl in particular?"

"No."

"Okay, thanks."

***

The other saloon he frequented was called The Buck-horn Saloon. The bartender's name was Morris, a tall, older man who looked like he'd been fired as the town undertaker.

"Ben Holden?" he said. "Yeah, he comes in here a lot."

"So he's a regular?"

"Yep."

"And he was in here today?"

"Today? No."

"Is that unusual? That he doesn't come in?" Clint asked.

"Not if he's workin'," the man said, wiping the bar with a dirty rag.

"Working? Doing what?"

The man shrugged.

"Whatever Holden does when he works," Morris said.

"Do you expect him tonight?" Clint asked.

"He'll either be here or go to the Union," Morris said.

"Can you tell me where he lives?"

"No."

"Can't, or won't?"

Morris stopped the circular motions he was making with the rag. "Can't," he said, "but even if I could, I wouldn't."

"You're afraid of him?" Clint asked.

"You bet I am," Morris said, "and you should be, too."

"Okay," Clint said, "just so I know, what's he look like?"

"He looks like the mean sonofabitch he is."

"That's it? That's all you've got to tell me?"

"Look," Morris said, "you keep that in mind, and you'll know 'im when you see 'im."

"How many guns does he wear?"

"One."

"Left side or right?"

Morris thought for a moment.

"Right."

"So I'm looking for a mean looking sonofabitch with a gun on his right hip."

"Now you've got it," Morris said.

"Thanks," Clint said. "Tell you what. I'll have a beer."

"Comin' up."

Morris set Clint up with a beer, which he nursed for a long time while he studied each man who entered the

59

saloon. By the time it was dark, he decided to switch venues.

"Thanks," he told Morris. "What do I owe you?"

"On the house," Morris said.

"I'll have more than one, next time," Clint promised.

"Let's hope there is a next time," Morris said.

Clint knew what he meant. The man was figuring he'd be killed by Ben Holden.

He left and walked over to the Union.

***

At The Union Saloon he ordered one beer and nursed it. He didn't want to have too many under his belt when he met Holden. Not after what everybody had told him. He knew the day was going to come when he finally met somebody faster than he was. He figured that day was still a long way off, but if it *was* Ben Holden, he didn't want to be drunk when it happened.

"Still lookin' for Holden?" Rex the bartender asked, as he set the beer down.

"That's right."

"Well, he ain't been in," Rex said, "but I expect him any time, now."

"You think I'll be able to get him to talk to me before he goes for his gun?" Clint asked.

"Holden ain't much of a talker," Rex said. "He likes action a lot better."

"I guess I'll just have to do the best I can, then," Clint commented.

"I wish ya luck," Rex said, and went to serve another patron.

Chapter Fifteen

Clint recognized Ben Holden as soon as he walked in. Even though they had never met, if he hadn't been told Holden was the meanest looking sonofabitch, he would've known him. He had both, the meanness and the look.

Clint waved to Rex.

"That him?"

"That's him. He's got a table in the back he always sits at."

Clint saw Holden walk across the floor, the other drinkers sitting at tables being sure not to meet his eye.

"Have a girl bring him a drink on me and tell him I'd like to talk to him," Clint said.

"Good idea," Rex said.

The bartender called over a cute blonde, gave her a beer and had her walk it over to Holden's table. She put the mug down and bent to speak into his ear. He kept his hand on her butt the whole time.

She came back to the bar and spoke to Rex, who walked over to Clint.

"He says come on over," Rex told him.

"Did she tell him who I am?"

"She did."

"I'll take a fresh beer, Rex," Clint said.

"Here," Rex said, "take two. He's happiest when he's drinkin'. Well, I think he's happy when he's killin', but drinkin's second."

"I'll keep that in mind. Thanks."

Clint picked up the beers and walked over. He held the two mugs in his left hand, keeping his gun hand free.

"You Adams?" Holden asked, as soon as he reached the table.

"I am."

"Have a seat." As Clint sat, Holden asked, "One of those for me?"

"It is."

Holden reached across the table and pulled it over to him, so that it was sitting next to the half-empty mug Clint had bought for him first.

"Stacy, the little blonde, says you been wantin' to talk to me today. Sorry I ain't been around."

"That's okay," Clint said. "Folks told me I'd find you in a saloon. I narrowed it down to this one and the Buck-horn."

"What's on your mind, then?" Holden asked.

"Constance Rayland."

"Who?"

"A girl who worked in the Depositor's Bank."

"I don't go to the bank," Holden said. "What about her?"

"She's missing."

"What's that gotta do with me?"

"She was last seen with you."

Holden stared across the table at Clint. His face was covered by dark stubble, but Clint could still see the scars beneath it. They twisted the man's mouth, hence his mean as hell look. He also had dead eyes that revealed nothing.

"Where?"

"In front of the Laramie Valley Hotel."

Holden finished his first beer, picked up the second.

"When was this?"

"Yesterday morning."

"Yesterday mornin'," Holden repeated. "I was in front of the hotel, yeah . . . and a woman bumped into me."

"I was told you grabbed her arm."

"Yeah, to keep her from fallin' over," Holden said. "I'm a mean sonofabitch, but I don't knock over women."

"I heard you grabbed her arm hard enough to hurt her."

"And I apologized," Holden said.

"And then where'd she go?"

Holden shrugged.

"I don't know," he said. "We went in separate directions."

"And you didn't see which way she went?"

"I went my way," Holden said, "she went hers."

Clint stared at him.

"Wait," Holden said. "You don't think I had somethin' to do with her goin' missin', do ya?"

"I'm just asking questions," Clint said.

"Now why would I have somethin' to do with her bein' missin'?" the gunman asked. "I don't even know her."

"You could've been hired to . . ."

"To . . . what?" Holden asked. "Kill 'er? I don't kill women."

"To grab her."

"And do what?"

"I don't know," Clint said. "Lock her up somewhere, maybe?"

"Look," Holden said, "I hire out my gun, or sometimes my fists, but I don't hire to snatch women off the street."

"Uh-huh," Clint said.

"So you better look someplace else."

"I don't even know where to start."

"Talk to the marshal," Holden suggested.

"He's useless."

"Sure, he is," Holden laughed. "But he's the law."

"Yeah, he is," Clint said. "Sorry to bother you."

"I hope you find 'er," Holden said. "Thanks for the beers."

"Thanks for your time."

Clint took his beer back to the bar.

"Get what you wanted?" Rex asked.

"Yes and no," Clint said. "Thanks for your help."

"Come on back," Rex said, as Clint turned and left.

Chapter Sixteen

After a quick breakfast the next morning Clint sat on the porch. He had come to Laramie to buy a saloon, not get involved in looking for a missing woman. It wasn't his fault she had disappeared, and it wasn't his responsibility to find her. What he should do was go to the bank and finish his negotiations with the bank manager, Mr. Edward. Buy the place for Rick, get it renovated, and make his final decision about the name of the place.

And find somebody to manage it.

That was plenty to do without having to look for a missing woman.

He left the porch to walk to the bank.

***

Ben Holden entered the room, put down the package he was carrying, then took the gag and blindfold off of Constance Rayland.

"Why are you doing this?" she demanded, her face streaked with dried tears.

"I don't know," he said. "I brought you some food."

"What do you mean, you don't know?" she asked.

He untied her hands.

"This ain't my idea. You can eat at the table."

"My feet are tied."

Holden lifted her up and carried her over to the chair in front of the table.

"There," he said. "Eat."

"You know Clint Adams is going to keep looking for me, don't you?"

"Also, not my problem or decision." He sat at the table across from her. "You're very pretty."

"Don't even think about touching me," she said, grabbing the fork on the table.

"I wouldn't," he said. "Just use that fork to eat, or I'll have to take it from you."

The meat on her plate was chicken and had been cut up for her so that she wouldn't need a knife.

"How long will you be keeping me here?" she asked.

"Until I'm told not to."

"Or until Clint Adams finds me," she added.

"He won't," Holden said. "I've already talked to him and convinced him I don't know where you are."

"And you think he believed you?"

"Yeah, I do."

Despite herself, Connie started to eat, as she found herself to be ravenously hungry.

Holden watched her eat, thinking she was a pretty thing for a bank girl. But he had been instructed to keep his hands off of her. So he watched her eat and waited for the chance to carry her back to her chair and tie her up . . .

***

Clint entered the bank and asked to see Mr. Edward. He was shown into the manager's office.

"Have you found Miss Rayland?" Edward asked, hopefully.

"No," Clint said, "but I've decided to go ahead and continue negotiating for The Bucket of Blood."

"Excellent," Mr. Edward said. "Will the marshal be looking for her?"

"I don't know," Clint said. "I'll still be looking if I get an idea of where to go, but for now, let's do this."

"All right," Edward said, rising, "let me get the file from Miss Rayland's desk . . ."

He left the room, returned with the file and sat back at his desk.

"Now, what was the last price you two discussed . . ."

***

They finally agreed on a price.

"How will you be paying for this, Mr. Adams?" Edward asked.

"I have a bank draft from my partner in Texas," Clint said, taking it from his pocket.

Edward took it and said, "This is an acceptable down payment. You and your partner certainly knew what price you wanted to pay and were ready."

"My partner's the money man," Clint said. "He told me what to do."

"Well," Edward said, "I'll file the papers, draw up the mortgage . . . I assume you have the authority to sign?"

"I do," Clint said. "I'll be a full partner in the place."

"Then you can sign here . . . and here . . . and I'll file the papers."

Clint finished signing and pushed the papers back across the desk.

"Can we do one more thing?" Edward asked.

"What's that?" Clint asked.

"I'd like to put a name on the paperwork," Edward said. "It won't necessarily be the final name, but it'll be something we can work with. Can we use The Bucket of Blood?"

"No," Clint said, thinking that Mr. Edward was trying to pull a fast one.

"What can we use, then?"

"Just put down," Clint said, "the Gunsmith Saloon."

Chapter Seventeen

"He wants to call it what?" the mayor asked.

"The Gunsmith Saloon," Edward said. "And he didn't say they were definitely going to call it that, but that's what he put down on the paperwork."

"'The Gunsmith Saloon,'" the mayor repeated. "Do you know the business that would bring to Laramie?"

"Well," Edward said, "to that saloon, yes."

"No," the mayor said, "I mean, it would bring people to town. They'd be in our hotels, our restaurants, our stores."

"So we're going ahead, then?" the bank manager asked.

The mayor looked at the paperwork on his desk, and at the bank draft for the down payment.

"Yes," he said, "for now we go ahead. Then I'll send some telegrams and find out who this Rick Hartman is."

"Okay," Edward said. "I'll get back to the bank."

He collected the paperwork from the mayor's desk and left the office. Another door opened to the mayor's right, and Ben Holden walked in.

"Let her go," the mayor said.

"What?"

"Let her go."

"And then what?" Holden asked.

"Tell her what will happen if she talks," the mayor said. "Put a good scare into her."

"And if she goes to the marshal?"

"I'll take care of the marshal," the mayor said.

"And what if she goes to the Gunsmith?"

"That would be a problem you'd have to deal with," the mayor said.

"If I kill 'im," Holden said, "what happens to your new saloon?"

"If you kill him," the mayor said, "people will come to Laramie to see the place the Gunsmith died. If you don't kill him, people will come here to go to the Gunsmith Saloon."

"Well, that's gonna be a hard decision for me," Holden said. "I wouldn't mind havin' the Gunsmith Saloon here in town, but I'd also like to be known as the man who killed the Gunsmith."

"Maybe," the mayor said, "we can do both."

***

"You can go," Holden said, untying Connie Rayland.

"What?" She was shocked. "Just like that?"

"Just like that," Holden said.

She stood up, unsteady on her feet because she had been seated so long.

"I can go right out the door?"

"Just walk out," Holden said. "There's only one thing."

"What?"

"If you go to the marshal, or tell Clint Adams that I was holding you, I'll have to kill both of you."

"Then what do I tell him?"

"You can tell your boss and Adams anythin' you want. Just not the truth. Unless you wanna deal with the consequences."

"But . . . what was this about?" she asked him.

"I don't even know," he said, "and I don't wanna know. My advice to you is to just go."

Connie almost thanked him, then remembered he was the one who grabbed her in the first place. She ran out the door. Realizing where she was, she started running toward town.

***

Clint was sitting on the porch of the hotel after supper, wondering if he had made the right decision in going forward with the purchase instead of continuing to search for Connie Rayland. He broke from his thoughts as he saw the bank manager, Mr. Edward, stepping up on the porch.

"I just closed the bank for the day," Edward said. "I thought I should tell you that Miss Rayland is there."

"She's back?" Clint asked. "Is she all right?"

"She seems fine."

"Where's she been?"

"She said she had something private to attend to," Edward said.

"Private?"

"A family matter."

"I thought she had no family here."

"That was what I thought, too," Edward said. "Apparently, I was wrong."

"What's she doing now?"

"Finishing up your paperwork for the purchase," Edward said. "By this time tomorrow, you'll be the new owner of The Bucket of Blood."

"The property that used to be The Bucket of Blood," Clint corrected.

"That's right," Edward said.

"All right," Clint said. "I'll come by the bank early tomorrow."

"See you then."

As Edward walked away, Clint wondered if he should go over to the bank to see Connie, but decided against it.

Maybe, when she was finished there, she would come to see him.

He settled down to wait.

Chapter Eighteen

When Connie didn't appear by dusk, Clint decided to walk to her house. When she opened the door to his knock, she didn't seem happy to see him.

"Connie," Clint said. "It's good to see you. I'm glad you're all right."

"I'm fine," she said. "I just had some . . . private business to take care of. I'm sorry I couldn't tell you before I left."

"Private business?"

"Just something to do with my family," she told him.

He thought of reminding her that she had told him she had no family, but decided against it. Maybe she was sending him a message.

"I heard you've talked with your boss," he said.

"Yes," she said, "you're going ahead with the purchase."

"That's right," he said. "I'll be at the bank in the morning."

"I'll see you there, then," she said.

"Yes," Clint said. "See you there."

She closed the door with no indication that she wanted him to come in. Something had happened to her, and she wasn't ready to talk about it. Clint was going to have to stick to business until she was.

***

In the morning Connie Rayland was at her desk when Clint entered the bank.

"Good morning," he said to her.

"Good morning, Clint," she said, not looking up. "Ready to sign?"

"I thought I did that yesterday, with Mr. Edward."

"He missed one or two things," she said. "Have a seat."

He sat across her desk from her.

"I've got some paperwork for you here," she said, loudly. Then she looked up at him and he could see the pleading in her eyes. "Make sure you read all the fine print."

He looked down at the paperwork. It was the same thing he had signed the day before, but at the bottom she had scrawled, "Help me. We need to talk."

"Okay," he said, signing the bottom and pushing the papers back to her.

"Can I do anything else for you?" she asked.

"Yes," he said, "you can take me over to the property again. I need to look over the inside before I hire some workers."

"I can do that," she said, still speaking loudly so everyone in the bank could hear. She opened her desk drawer and took out some keys. "We can walk over there right now, if that's convenient."

"I've got nothing else to do," he said. "Let's go."

They both stood up and left the bank.

"Connie—" he started, as they walked.

"Not yet," she said, shortly.

They reached The Bucket of Blood and she used the keys to unlock the front door. Once they were inside, she closed and locked it behind them, then turned and fell against him. He put his arms around her, felt her trembling.

"What's going on, Connie?" he asked.

"I need a minute," she said. "Just hold me . . . tighter."

He squeezed her tightly. They stood that way a while, and then she stepped away.

"I was grabbed off the street, tied up, gagged and held in a small shack outside of town," she said. "I was given water and food, then tied and gagged again."

"And why was this done?"

"I don't know."

"You were never told?"

"The man who took me didn't know, either," she said. "He was just hired to do it."

"That's what he told you?"

"Yes."

"How did you get away?"

"I didn't get away," she said. "He let me go."

"Okay," Clint said, "who was it? Who took you?"

She bit her lip, then said, "I—I can't tell you that."

"Why not?"

"I was warned."

"Then why are we here?" Clint asked. "Why are we talking now?"

"I—I just wanted you to know that I . . . I wasn't mad at you, or anything. I—I just can't talk to you about this."

"So you've been threatened into keeping quiet?" he asked.

"Yes."

"If you talk, he'll kill you?"

"And whoever I talk to," she said. "I—I can't risk that."

"From what I know of this town," he said, "that means one person to me. Was it Ben Holden?"

Her eyes went wide.

"I can't tell you!" she said. "I can't." She grabbed for the door, unlocked it. "Just know this is nothing against you!"

"Connie!" he yelled, but she opened the door and ran out.

Chapter Nineteen

Clint had meant to ask the bank—Miss Rayland, or Mr. Edward—for recommendations when it came to carpenters and such. However, it didn't seem like Connie was anxious to be seen with him.

He could go back to the saloons he had already patronized and talk to the bartenders—Rex, and Morris—about those kinds of workers. The only other people he had spoken to were the marshal and the mayor, and he didn't relish going back to either one of them.

Since he was inside the building at the moment, he decided to walk around at his leisure and have a good look at each room, and each floor, to decide just how much work needed to be done.

He spent the next few hours doing that, including walking the stage to see if it needed work, and checking out the rooms on the second floor.

The bar itself seemed to be in good, solid shape. It probably just needed to be sanded and repainted, but the structure of it seemed sound.

After three hours, he had an idea of what needed to be done. Rick Hartman might have seen more if he was there, but that wasn't going to happen. At least, not until the place was in full swing, which would be months away. Clint wasn't going to be able to stay in Laramie all that time. He would have to get the work going, and then return later to see the finished product.

That meant finding someone he could trust and hiring them to oversee the work. That, in itself, would take time.

Of course, he could import someone to do the job, but he'd have to send many telegrams in order to find the best person. It would be faster to hire someone locally.

He had no idea how long those kinds of interviews would take, so he had to get started.

He left The Bucket of Blood and headed for the Union Saloon . . .

***

Rex smiled as Clint stepped up to The Union House bar.

"Beer?"

"Sure," Clint said. "It's late enough in the afternoon."

Rex set him up.

"Looks like you found Holden and things went well?" Rex said. "You're both still walkin' around."

"That may be temporary," Clint said. "We're going to talk again, but until we do, I have another favor to ask."

Rex leaned on the bar and said, "Go ahead. I've got nothing better to do, until we get busy.

There were only two other customers in the place, each seated at their own table.

"I need some carpenters," Clint said. "I'm going to need a lot of work done."

"I heard the sale of the Bucket went through," Rex said. "I can recommend a few people."

"Good. I'll talk to them all. I'd like to have a choice."

Rex reeled off three names and gave Clint some background on all of them. Clint decided to go and talk to them all immediately.

He finished his beer, thanked Rex, and left The Union.

***

The first name was Lance Bannister. According to Rex, Bannister had worked on the new church, if Clint wanted to go and see a sample of his work. So Clint stopped by the church first and liked what he saw, then followed Rex's directions to the man's shop.

It was on a side street, and as Clint entered, he was surprised at the mess. Apparently, the man saved his quality work for his customers.

"Damn!" he heard as he walked in, followed by some cursing coming from a back room.

"Hello? Mr. Bannister?"

A fat man in his fifties came through a door, sucking on the thumb of his right hand. He was red-faced, but that might not have been his usual look.

"Just call me Lance," he said, around the thumb. "Sorry, you walked in just when I hammered my own damned thumb. Damn it!" He shook the hand and then stuck the digit back into his mouth. "What can I do for you?"

"You're the man who did the work on the church?" Clint asked.

"That's right."

Clint looked around doubtfully, and then back at the fat man.

"I know," Bannister said, "I don't look the part, but the church, that's my work. This," he waved his hands, "is just my workshop."

"I get it," Clint said.

"What's the job?"

"I bought The Bucket of Blood," Clint said. "It needs some renovating before I can open it."

"You're gonna reopen the Bucket?" Bannister asked, surprised.

"Not as The Bucket of Blood," Clint said. "My partner and me, we're giving it a new name."

"Wow," Bannister said. "A lot of people in town ain't gonna like that."

"What about you?"

"Me?" Bannister said. "I'd love the work. You talk to anybody else in town about it?"

"I've got three names," Clint said. "You're the first I'm talking to."

"Well," Bannister said, "talk to the other two, and then let me know. I'll give you a good price."

"Don't you want to know the other names?"

"I've gotta good idea who they'll be," Bannister said. "We're all good at our jobs, but you make up your mind and then let me know."

"Okay," Clint said, as Bannister sucked on his thumb again. "I hope your finger's okay."

"Occupational hazard," Bannister told him. "It'll be black-and-blue, but I've got nine more. I'll be ready to go when you are."

"I'll get back to you," Clint said, and left.

Chapter Twenty

The second carpenter's name was Joe Spencer.

Rex hadn't told Clint about any samples of the man's work, so Clint simply followed the directions to his shop. Spencer turned out to be a small man in his forties, with a very clean workplace.

"The Bucket of Blood?" he asked. "That's been abandoned for years."

"I know," Clint said. "That's why it needs work."

"Well, I'd have to look at it in order to come up with a price," Spencer said, "but it sounds like an expensive proposition."

"That's what I thought."

"Have you spoken to other carpenters?"

"I've talked to one other, and still have a third to see," Clint said.

"So you'll be choosing from the three of us, once we all give you a price?"

"It looks that way."

"We'll all have to take a look at the property," Spencer said, "even though we're familiar with The Bucket of Blood."

"After I've talked to the third name on my list, I'll arrange a time for all of us to meet there."

"That suits me," Spencer sad. "I'd like to see who my competition is, even though I have an idea."

"I'll let you know by the day's end when we should meet," Clint said.

"I'll be waiting."

Clint turned and left, heading for the shop of the third carpenter.

***

The third carpenter was a young man in his twenties, named Winston Stark. He had a shop on West Ivinson Street. As Clint entered, he saw many samples of the man's work around him, mostly furniture.

"Can I help you?" the young man asked, from behind the counter.

"Mr. Stark?"

"At your service."

Clint explained what he wanted, and that there were three possibilities, Stark being one of them.

"Ah, I heard that property had been purchased," Stark said. He sounded like he had been educated back East. "I'd relish a chance at that job."

"Good," Clint said. "Can you meet me there in two hours?"

"Sure," Stark said, "will the others be there?"

"I'm going to see them now," Clint said. "I think they'll come."

The young man smiled.

"Then I'll see you all in two hours.

***

Clint had to go to the bank again to get a key from Connie, as she hadn't left him one when they were together earlier that morning.

"There you go," she said, handing him a set. "Keys to everything."

"Thank you, Connie," Clint said.

Connie Rayland looked away nervously and said, "You're welcome."

He wished they could talk again, but this wasn't the place for it, so he just turned and left, headed over to The Bucket of Blood.

Chapter Twenty-One

Clint got to The Bucket of Blood before the three carpenters. They then arrived one at a time, knocking on the door. First Stark, then Spencer and, finally, Bannister.

Stark and Spencer shook hands, and then, when Bannister entered, he started to laugh.

"I figured it'd be you two."

This time they all shook hands.

"Okay," Clint said, "you've got the run of the place. Take a look around."

"Well, right from here I can see the bar needs work," Bannister said.

"How's the structural integrity?" Stark asked.

"'Structural integrity?'" Bannister repeated. "Jesus."

"The bar is sound," Clint said.

Spencer kept quiet, but walked over to the bar and knocked on it.

"Sounds good," Stark said.

Clint took a seat while the three men walked back and forth, up and down, inspecting every inch of the place.

One-by-one they came back to the main room and sat down with him.

"Nothin' to drink?" Bannister asked. "I thought this was a saloon."

"Not yet," Clint said. "If we make a deal we can go over to The Union for a beer."

"Sounds good," Spencer said.

"So what do you say?" Clint asked.

The three men looked at each other and seemed to wordlessly decide who would go first.

"The basic structure is sound," Stark said. "The bar needs to be sanded and painted, floorboards need to be replaced on the stage and main floor."

"A lot of it's cleaning," Bannister added. "Getting rid of the grime and the years."

"I saw some leaks upstairs," Spencer said. "Somebody's gonna have to work on the roof."

"Can one of you do that, or do I need . . . what? A roofer?" Clint asked.

The three carpenters looked at each other.

"This is a big job," Bannister said. "If one of us gets it, he'd have to hire help."

"But if the three of us work together," Spencer said, "we can split the responsibilities."

"I can do the roof," Stark said.

"I can do the cleanup part," Bannister said. He saw Clint looking at him. "What? I can be clean."

"I can do the bar and the boards, work on strengthening some of the walls," Stark said.

"I have no objection to you three working together," Clint said. "As long as I get one price."

"We can work on that," Stark said. He looked at the other two. "What do you say?"

"I'm in," Spencer said.

"Me, too," Bannister said. "But who's in charge?"

Stark pointed at Clint and said, "He is."

"I can live with that," Spencer said.

"So can I," Bannister said.

"When can you start?" Clint asked.

"We have to get the paint and wood," Stark said. "That'll take a few days. While we're waiting, I can start the sanding."

"And I can start cleaning," Bannister said.

"I'll go up on the roof and see exactly what has to be done," Spencer said.

"We'll need some money up front, for supplies," Stark said.

"First I need your final price," Clint told them. "I can have some money tomorrow."

"We'll come up with a price by tomorrow," Spencer said. "Right, boys?"

Bannister and Stark nodded.

"Have you fellas worked together before?" Clint asked.

"On occasion," Stark said. "When the job was big enough."

"Like this one," Spencer said.

"Well then," Clint said, standing up, "let's go over to The Union and seal it with a beer."

"Sounds good to me!" Bannister said, cheerfully.

The other two nodded and they all left, with Clint locking the door behind them.

***

The Union was pretty busy, and instead of trying to find room for four at the bar, they took a table. Clint offered to go get the beers.

"Looks like you made some new friends," Rex said, setting the beers in front of him.

"Business acquaintances," Clint corrected, picking up the four mugs.

The three carpenters had grabbed a table in the middle of the room, but Clint said, "Let's go over there," and led them to a table against the wall. He set the four beers down and sat.

"Here's to The Bucket of Blood," Bannister said, raising his glass.

"It's not going to be called that," Clint said.

"So what do we drink to, then?" Spencer asked.

"Yes," Stark said, "what's it going to be called?"

Clint thought the three men should know who they were working for, in case it made a difference.

"For now," he said, "let's just call it The Gunsmith Saloon."

The three men stared at him, and Bannister asked, "Why would we call it that?"

Chapter Twenty-Two

Clint had one beer with the three carpenters, then bought them another round and left them to figure out their finances.

He was walking to the batwing doors when they swung in and Ben Holden entered.

"Adams," Holden said. "You headin' out. Come on, I'll buy you one."

"Why not?" Clint said.

They went to the bar, where several men moved out of the way, either because it was Holden, the Gunsmith, or both.

Rex set two beers on the bar and walked away.

"I'm letting you buy me this beer because I want to talk to you, Holden."

"Yeah? About what?"

"Constance Rayland."

"I told you before, I don't know the girl. I don't go to her bank. Just bumped into her, apologized, and left."

"Well, she went missing for a day, and says a man tied and gagged her, and then let her go."

"So?"

"Was it you?"

"Did she say it was me?" Holden asked.

"No," Clint said, "she won't say who it was because she's scared."

"Well, it wasn't me."

"Who else would she be scared of, Holden?" Clint asked. "Aren't you the scariest man in town?"

Holden studied Clint for a few moments, then turned to face him head on.

"Yeah," he said, "I probably am the scariest man in Laramie, but didn't know nothin' about her the last time you asked, and I don't know nothin' now. Why are you askin' me about her, again?"

"Because I think it was you," Clint said. "I think you grabbed her, held her, and then let her go after scaring the hell out of her."

"You think I pick on girls?" Holden asked.

"I think you pick on anybody you're paid to pick on," Clint said.

"Oh, so now you think somebody paid me to grab her?"

"From what I've heard, you don't do anything without getting paid."

"Then you better hope nobody pays me to come after you, huh?"

"No," Clint said, "I think you better hope nobody hires you to come after me." He put his beer down and got into Holden's face. "Or that Connie Rayland doesn't come around and tell me it was you who grabbed her."

He walked away without another word.

***

"You don't touch him," the mayor said, later that day.

"You mean, not until he gets his place up and runnin', right?"

"No," the mayor said, "I mean, at all. I'm not hiring you to kill the Gunsmith, Holden."

"Maybe you won't have to," Holden said. "Killin' him would be good for my reputation. To hell with your town."

"Look," the mayor said, "I made a mistake using you to grab that girl. I wasn't convinced it was a good idea for The Bucket of Blood to reopen, but then I met with the town council. They were pretty much all for it, and I saw the error of my ways. I'm not going to be using you for any more jobs."

Holden stared at the man.

"You can go," the mayor said.

"When did you get to be such a brave man, Mr. Mayor, talkin' to me like that?" Holden asked. "I could put a bullet in you right now and walk away."

"But you won't," the mayor said.

"Why not?"

The mayor leaned back in his chair.

"Because nobody's paying you."

The mayor had his hand on the top drawer of his desk. Inside the draw was a Navy Colt that had belonged to his father. He didn't know if he'd be able to get it out in time. Then, when Ben Holden turned and headed for the door, he opened the drawer with intentions of shooting the man in the back. It seemed to be the only way to get rid of him and fixing the mistake he'd made by using him in the first place.

As he cocked back the hammer on the colt, Holden turned, drew and fired once. The bullet hit the mayor in the center of the forehead, snapping his head back. He sat in his chair as if pinned to it for a few moments, then slid to the floor.

The outer office had been empty when Holden arrived. He stuck his head around the door to make sure it still was. Then he holstered his gun and proceeded to ransack the office, making it look as if a desperate struggle had taken place. The mayor was the last of the Moyer clan, who had owned The Bucket of Blood. They had all been hanged, so maybe nobody would question the fact that Mayor Long had died violently.

He left the mayor where he was, on the floor behind his desk with the Navy Colt by his side.

Chapter Twenty-Three

Clint was sitting on the hotel porch after supper, having left the three carpenters at The Union Saloon. But he had a sudden thought that brought him to his feet and propelled him back to the saloon.

Rex was busy behind the bar, and it looked like the three carpenters were gone. That suited Clint, since it was the bartender he had come to see.

"Back so soon?" Rex asked, when he saw him.

"Do you have time to talk?" Clint asked.

"Not right now, but stay and have a beer. As soon as I can I'll come and join you."

Rex put a beer on the bar.

"Thanks," Clint said. "I'll be in the back."

"As soon as I get somebody to spell me here, we'll talk."

Clint nodded, walked through the crowded room to a back table and sat. He nursed the beer and watched the activity around him until Rex appeared less than an hour later.

"Doesn't look like it's slowed down any," Clint said, as Rex sat.

"It hasn't, but I've got somebody behind the bar. What's goin' on?"

"I've got the carpenters getting ready to work on the new Bucket of Blood," Clint said.

"That's good," Rex said.

"But when the place is ready, I'm going to need somebody to run it."

Rex stared at Clint, as if waiting for him to say more, then seemed to get it.

"You mean, me?"

"If you want the job."

"I've got a job," Rex said.

"Do you run this place?" Clint asked.

"No, I'm just the head bartender."

"Well, in my place you'll be the manager," Clint told him. "You'll be running the whole show."

"And reporting to you?"

"Me and my partner, Rick Hartman, but neither of us will be around much, so mostly you'll be on your own."

"Do I get to hire my staff?"

"You'll have to," Clint said. "I don't know anybody in town but you."

"I make pretty good money here," Rex said.

"We'll double it" Clint said.

That shocked Rex.

"Jesus, what're ya gonna call this place?"

"That's still open to discussion between me and my partner," Clint said, "but Rick wants to call it the Gunsmith Saloon."

"I'm in," Rex said, right away. The two men shook hands. "When do I start?"

"Well, for now hold on to this job, but keep an eye on the work as it's being done on the place. I'm using all three of those carpenters whose names you gave me."

"They'll do good work," Rex said.

"It's going to be up to you to see that they do," Clint said. "When you have time, you can walk over there with me and look things over. I'm sure my partner will also be sending me suggestions."

"Now, you're redoin' the whole place, right?" Rex asked. "Including the upstairs rooms."

"That's right," Clint said, "but I doubt we'll be using those rooms the same way The Bucket of Blood did."

"But you are gonna have girls, right?" Rex asked.

"Right," Clint said. "And good looking ones."

"I'll do my best to find 'em." Rex smiled. "You can count on that."

Rex went back to work behind the bar, while Clint finished off his beer. In the morning he would telegraph Rick that he found their manager. He knew that would be when Rick started sending telegrams back with suggestions and/or demands. For one thing, Clint knew Rick was going to want some crystal in the place, possibly chandeliers.

He got up and left The Union, tossing a wave Rex's way, which the bartender returned as a salute.

***

When Clint entered the lobby of the Laramie Valley Inn, he saw Marshal July Jackson leaning against the front desk, apparently waiting for him.

"Finally," Jackson said, "I've been waiting for hours."

"I bet you could've found me in a saloon if you tried," Clint said.

Jackson looked around, then took hold of Clint's left arm and pulled him away from the desk.

"I didn't want to talk to you in a saloon, and I don't wanna do it here, in the lobby. Can we go to your room?"

"We can if you tell me what this is about," Clint answered.

The marshal looked around again, then lowered his voice and said, "I found the mayor dead in his office a few hours ago. He was shot."

"Let's go to my room," Clint said.

Chapter Twenty-Four

When they got to Clint's room, Jackson asked, "Do you have anythin' to drink?"

"No."

"I guess we shoulda gone to my office, then."

"Never mind that," Clint said. "Tell me about the mayor."

"Somebody shot him," Jackson said. "In his office."

"How?"

"It looks like there was a struggle. I found him lying behind his desk with a bullet hole in his forehead. Next to him on the floor was an unfired Navy Colt."

"Did anybody come forward as a witness?"

"I, uh, haven't really told anyone about this, yet."

"What? Where's the body?"

"Still in his office."

"Nobody else saw anything?"

"No," Jackson said.

"Why haven't you at least taken him to the undertaker?" Clint asked.

"Look," Jackson said, "I don't know what do, here. I thought maybe you'd take a look at . . . you know, everythin'."

"All right," Clint said. "Let's go."

"Now?"

"Right now," Clint said. "Take me over there."

"Let me ask you one thing, first," Jackson said.

"Like what?"

"Did you shoot him?"

"No."

"Okay," Jackson said, "Let's go."

***

When Clint entered the mayor's office, he saw what the marshal meant. There was a lot of carnage—almost too much.

"Staged," he said.

"What?"

"This was staged," Clint said. "There was no fight."

"Look at this mess," Jackson said.

"I know," Clint said. "There's too much of it."

"So you don't think there was a fight?"

"No," Clint said. "I think somebody just shot him."

"Who'd do that?" Jackson asked.

"You're asking me?" Clint asked. "How about Ben Holden."

"Why would Holden shoot the mayor?" Jackson asked. "He only does what he's paid to do."

"So, somebody paid him."

"Can't be," Jackson said. "When Long won, it was by a landslide. Everybody loves 'im. This is gonna be too much for this town to take."

"Well," Clint said, "you're going to have to tell them."

"Jesus," Jackson said, "How am I gonna do that?"

"Is there a town council?"

"Yeah, there is."

"You might start there, then," Clint suggested. "For now, why don't you go and get the undertaker while I take a look around."

"Yeah, okay," the marshal said. "He's down the street, so I'll be right back."

While the lawman was gone, Clint went around behind the desk and crouched down by the mayor. He picked up the Navy Colt, sniffed it and checked the loads. It was fully loaded, but hadn't been fired and reloaded.

The top drawer of the desk was open, leading Clint to believe that was where the Colt had been. Whoever shot the mayor, the politician hadn't been able to get his gun out in time.

He went back around the desk to sit in the visitor's chair and wait for the lawman and the undertaker.

***

When the two men arrived, the dour man in a dark coat walked around behind the desk to look at his new charge. Marshal Jackson stood beside the still seated Clint.

"Who would do something like this," the undertaker said, shaking his head.

"That's for your marshal to figure out," Clint said.

Jackson gave Clint a quick look.

The undertaker bent over the body, then straightened.

"I should get the doc, and a few men to carry him out," he said. "I'll be back."

"We'll be here," Jackson assured him.

After the undertaker left, Clint stood up and said, "Why should I wait here?"

"I know this is my job, Adams, but I ain't no detective," Jackson said.

"You don't have to be," Clint said. "There's a town council. See what they have to offer."

"And then what?"

"The mayor got somebody sore at him," Clint said. "Just see what the town council has to say and go from there. I've got work to do."

Clint left the office, and the befuddled looking lawman.

Chapter Twenty-Five

In the morning Clint met all the carpenters at the site of the new Gunsmith Saloon, after sending a telegram to Rick Hartman. He waited just outside the office for a reply, and it came in shortly.

Rick's telegram said: SOUNDS GREAT. STAY AS LONG AS YOU CAN. AND DON'T FORGET SOME CRYSTAL.

"Crystal" Clint said, tucking the missive away in his pocket, "predictable."

When he got to the site, the three men were waiting outside.

"Good-morning," he said.

"'mornin'," Bannister said. "I got a buckboard out in back."

"I'll go in and open the back door for you," Clint said, unlocking the front.

Stark and Spencer entered with him, while Bannister went around back to wait. Clint walked through to the back door and unlocked it.

"Thanks," the heavy man said. "We figured we could use this storeroom for our supplies. That okay?"

"That's fine."

Stark came through to help Bannister unpack. They pulled the tarp off the buckboard bed.

"Where's Spencer?" Clint asked.

"He's up on the roof, already," Stark said. "Walkin' around tryin' to figure out what's what."

Clint stepped aside, allowing Bannister and Stark to carry in some long boards that were belted together into a heavy bundle.

"Hello?" Somebody shouted from the front.

"I'll check that out," Clint said. "Keep unloading."

As he entered the saloon, he saw Rex standing just inside the front door.

"There you are," the bartender said. "I thought I'd take a look over here before I opened up The Union."

"Have you ever been in here?" Clint asked. "I mean, while it was still open?"

"No," Rex said. "I'm a little too young to remember the Bucket when it was in full swing."

"Well then," Clint said, "have a look."

Rex walked around the room, looked at the stage, then went to the bar and put his hands on it.

"This is sturdy," he said. "Needs a little work, but your carpenters can see to that."

"And they will."

Rex came back around.

"I better get The Union open," he said. "This place will be . . . fantastic, won't it?"

"I hope so," Clint said.

"I'll check in when I can with Stark, Bannister and Spencer."

"Good."

"See ya later, boss."

As Rex left, Spencer came down the stairs from the second level.

"How's the roof?" Clint asked.

"I don't think it'll leak when it rains, but it does need some patching up. Also, that railing up there needs to be enforced. Right now, if someone leaned on it, they'd end up down here."

None of the carpenters had mentioned hearing that the mayor had been killed. Clint assumed Marshal Jackson was still keeping it quiet. He hoped the lawman would heed his advice and meet with the town council. Somebody should know what the mayor was up to. And they should also know if the mayor made a habit of paying Ben Holden for work. The two may have had a falling out, possibly over what happened with Constance Rayland.

Clint checked the storeroom, saw that it had been filled with the supplies from the buckboard.

"Here you go," Bannister said, handing Clint a piece of paper.

"What's this?" Clint asked.

"That's the bill for the supplies, so far," the big man said.

"You laid this money out?"

"The places we do business with let us buy on credit," Bannister explained. "But we'd like to pay them as soon as possible."

"I'll have the cash for you this afternoon."

"Good enough," Bannister said. "I'll tell the others."

Clint folded the bill and stuck it in his pocket, figuring it was going to be the first of many.

He stuck around until later in the afternoon, then left to go to the bank before it closed. He withdrew the money for the bill in his pocket, plus some extras so the carpenters wouldn't have to use their own credit again.

He went back to the saloon, found Bannister in the back and handed him the money. Someone inside the building was heard hammering.

"That's Spencer on the roof," Bannister said.

"Where's Stark?"

"We found a root cellar," Bannister said. "He's checkin' that out."

"Good to know," Clint said.

Stark entered, his face smudged with dirt from the root cellar, and said to Clint, "The law's out front, Clint. Don't know what you did."

"Thanks, Stark. I'll go see what the marshal wants."

Chapter Twenty-Six

Clint found Marshal Jackson waiting for him just inside the door.

"What's on your mind, Marshal?" Clint asked. "I haven't heard the news come out about the mayor, yet."

"I met with the town council, like you suggested," Jackson said. "They wanna keep it quiet as long as we can."

"Anybody on the council give you something to work with?" Clint asked.

"They're all afraid to say," Jackson said, "but I could tell they were thinkin' about Holden."

"So, are you going to brace him?"

"It's my job," Jackson said, "but I could use some backup."

"No deputies?"

"A couple of part-timers," Jackson said, "but they won't do the trick."

"And I will?"

"Well . . . Holden's a gunman, so are you. I'm just a badge-toter."

"What about a new mayor?" Clint asked. "Anybody stepping up?"

"Not until we find out who killed Mayor Long," Jackson said. "Nobody wants to step up if somebody's just killin' mayors."

"So what do you want me to do?" Clint asked.

"Just stand with me when I question Holden," Jackson said. I doubt he'll draw on both of us."

"Okay, I'll do it," Clint said, "as long as I don't have to wear a badge."

"That's okay with me," Jackson said. "I just want some backup."

"You've got it," Clint said. "Just tell me when."

"I'll let you know."

As the lawman left, Clint pondered his decision. He wasn't in a hurry to back the lawman up on any play, but he did want to face Ben Holden again and talk to him about Connie. And he had also decided to talk to Connie again, now that he had men working on the saloon, and had hired a manager.

He told the carpenters he would see them again in the morning.

"Lock up when you leave," he told Bannister, handing him an extra key that had been in with the others.

"Thanks," Bannister said, pocketing the key. "We will."

***

Clint walked to the bank and positioned himself across the street. He knew Connie wouldn't be comfortable with him inside, so he decided to simply wait for her to come out.

The bank closed at five. He watched as two tellers exited and headed home, and then an older woman who sat at one of the desks came out. Finally, Connie appeared and started walking. Clint decided to follow her home and reveal himself there.

By following her, he was able to be certain that he was the only one. When they reached her house, he allowed her to go inside and close the door before he crossed the street and went up the walk. He knocked and waited.

When she opened the door, she looked at him in surprise, then reached out and pulled him inside.

"I don't want anyone to see you," she said, desperately. "Why are you here?"

"The mayor was killed last night," Clint said.

"What? How?"

"Shot to death in his office."

"Oh my God!" she breathed. "Who did it?"

"Nobody knows for sure," Clint said, "but maybe you can help."

"Me? How?"

"I have a feeling I know who did it."

"Who?"

"The same man who grabbed you and held you for a day," he said. "All you have to do is tell me who that was."

"Oh God . . ." she said, sitting down in a chair as if she had lost the strength in her legs.

"Come on, Connie," Clint said. "I know he threatened you, and I know you're scared. But the only way we can take that fear away is for you to tell me his name."

"Will you kill him?"

"Not if I don't have to," Clint said. "The marshal wants to talk to him."

"And what if he kills you?" she asked. "How am I supposed to feel, then?"

"You shouldn't worry about that," he told her. "You just do your part by telling me who he is, and I'll take care of the rest."

She rubbed both hands over her face, left them there for a few seconds, then dropped them away.

"Connie . . ."

She stared into his eyes and he could see all the fear there.

"It was Ben Holden," she said.

Chapter Twenty-Seven

"What will you do now?" she asked.

"The marshal and I will go and talk to Holden," Clint said.

"Are you going to tell him I told you?" she asked.

"No," he said. "He won't find out from me."

She breathed a sigh of relief.

"Can you stay?" she asked.

"No," Clint said, "I have to go talk to Marshal Jackson."

"And you'll talk to Holden tonight?" she asked, wringing her hands.

"That remains to be seen," he said. "It might be tomorrow. But until we get that done, I'm going to stay away from you."

"That's probably best," she agreed. "But you have to let me know what happens."

"I will."

He gave her a hug, then went to the front door and peered out. When he was certain there was nobody around, he went out the door and headed back to the center of town.

***

"So it *was* him," Marshal Jackson said.

Clint was sitting in a chair in front of Jackson's desk, and he nodded.

"But I promised her we wouldn't let him know she'd identified him."

"Then how do we play it?" Jackson asked.

"You don't want to arrest him for holding her captive for a day," Clint said, "you want him for killing the mayor."

"But we know he held her," Jackson said. "We don't know that he killed the mayor."

"Let's see if we can make him believe that we do know," Clint said, "and then get him to admit to it."

"Tonight?" Jackson asked.

"No, to do it tonight, we'd have to do it in a saloon, where he might have friends," Clint said. "Let's find him tomorrow. That'll give you tonight to figure out your approach."

"My first thought," Jackson said, "is to shoot him in the back."

"You'd be surprised how many men would still be alive if they did that," Clint said. "Many men think that's a smart play when facing somebody better than they are with a gun."

"But not you, huh?" Jackson asked.

"I've never been that desperate," Clint said. "And I hate backshooters."

"Yeah, I figured you'd say that."

"I'll meet you back here in the morning," Clint said. "Remember, you're in charge and I'm just backing your play."

"Yeah, right," Jackson said, with no enthusiasm.

As Clint left the office, he hoped the lawman wouldn't just take off his badge and leave town.

***

When Clint entered the lobby of his hotel, he was surprised to find somebody waiting to see him. He had a feeling that now the renovations had begun on the old Bucket of Blood, this would be happening more and more.

The woman was tall and slender, wearing a nicer dress than the last time he had seen her. She had also fixed her hair and her face, so that she didn't look as if she had just come from work.

"You don't recognize me, do you?" she demanded.

"Sure I do," he said. "You're the lady who has a shop across the street from the, uh, Bucket of Blood. Mrs. Wells, Right? Abby?"

She looked impressed.

"You do remember."

"I don't forget attractive women," he said. "What can I do for you?"

"I want to talk to you about . . . that place," she said. "Can we go somewhere?"

"Would you like to get a drink—"

"No, I don't want to go to a saloon," she said. "Can we go to your room?"

He was surprised at that suggestion.

"Um . . ." he started.

"If you're worried about my reputation, don't," she said. "I don't care much what people in this town think of me."

"Look, Mrs. Wells—"

"Just call me Abby," she said.

"Okay, Abby—"

"All right if I call you Clint?"

"That's fine, but—"

"Come on, Clint," she said. "I don't have all day. Lead the way to your room."

"Yes, Ma'am," he said, finally. "This way."

They walked to the stairs and he said, "After you."

Following her up the stairs, he watched as the fabric of her dress moved and was suddenly aware that she was wearing nothing under the dress.

Or was it his imagination?

Chapter Twenty-Eight

It wasn't.

As they reached his room, she stood aside so he could unlock the door. Then he allowed her to go in first. By the time he locked the door and turned to face her, her dress was on the floor.

"Okay, look," she said, which was exactly what he was doing, "it's been a while since I've been with a man. The pickin's in this town are real slim."

"Why choose me?" he asked.

"When I first saw you, I thought you were handsome," she said. "Then I heard who you are. That's when I decided, you're the man."

"Abby—"

"Oh, don't try to tell me you don't want me," she scolded him. "I see the way you're lookin' at me."

She was tall and lean, with small breasts topped with dark nipples. Her skin was smooth and pale, and although she was probably over forty, she was extremely desirable. That wasn't the problem.

"Abby, I don't really have time—"

"Sure you do," she said. Her hair was in a bun. She reached up and released it. It fell down past her shoulders in waves. "What else have you got to do?"

"Well," he said, at a loss for words, "I was going to have supper."

"Eat later, Mr. Gunsmith," she said. "Bed me now."

"Yes, Ma'am."

He started to unbutton his shirt as she crawled onto the bed.

"I've got one question," he said, tossing his shirt aside and starting to undo his pants.

"What's that?"

"Are you still going to complain about my saloon after this?"

"Oh, yes . . ." she breathed, but it might have been because he dropped his pants and his hard penis came into sight . . .

***

Ben Holden wondered what his next move should be?

Word had not yet spread about the mayor's death. The body couldn't still be in his office. It had to have been found by now and moved to the undertaker's. That meant it was being kept quiet on purpose. Whatever the plan was, he had to act natural, as if nothing had happened. That was what he was thinking when he walked into The Union Saloon that night.

There was no way anybody could prove he had killed Mayor Long.

***

Marshal July Jackson wanted a drink, but he didn't want to run into Ben Holden that night in a saloon. He went to the hotel room the town supplied him with and took a bottle of whiskey from the bottom drawer of the chest he used for his meager belongings.

He sat down on the worn sofa, uncapped the bottle and took a drink. Was the town really paying him enough to go up against the likes of Ben Holden?

He answered that question by taking another drink.

***

Clint usually preferred big nipples on large breasts. Abby had them on her small breasts, and he found it oddly mesmerizing. Or it was the way she had tricked him into taking her to his room.

Or a combination of both.

On any case, he spent an inordinate amount of time with her nipples in his mouth, which she didn't seem to mind. She cradled his head there and cooed to him while he sucked her. When he slid his hand down between her legs, she began to writhe around and moan out loud. Suddenly she stopped moving and he looked down at her, afraid she had passed out.

"Are you okay?"

"Oh yeah Mr. Adams," she said, with a dreamy smile. "I just thought I might enjoy this even more if I wasn't flopping around."

"Do you want to take a break?" he asked.

"Hell, no!" she said. "I've never had a man spend so much time on me before."

"Well, I wouldn't get used to it," Clint said, "at least, not after tonight."

"I'm only concerned with tonight," she told him. "Continue, please."

He went back to work on her . . .

***

She may have wanted to lie still and enjoy, but later, when his face was pressed to her crotch and he was probing through her pubic patch with his tongue, she began to drum her heels on the mattress, uncontrollably.

"Oh God!" she cried out, reaching for him. "Oh Jesus, you're so damn good at that!"

He accepted the compliment by continuing.

Oooooh," she moaned, after taking it as long as she could. She reached for him and said, "Can you come up here . . . please?"

He obeyed, taking his mouth from her vagina and moving up next to her. She put her arms around him and pulled him onto her, kissing him. Then she slid her hands between them so she could grab his cock.

"Oh lord," she said, "let's get that beautiful thing inside me."

"You're kind of bossy," he said, "but okay."

With a jerk of his hips, he was inside her. Her eyes went wide, a look of rapture took over her face. He began to move in and out of her, staring down at her suddenly beautiful face.

"Oh yes," she moaned out loud, "Oh my God, yes, go faster . . . faster . . .

He slid his hands beneath her, cupped her ass in his hands, and gave her what she was asking for. He went faster and faster until, finally, he was yelling right along with her . . .

Chapter Twenty-Nine

Abby Wells laid in bed with the sheet wrapped around her, while Clint got dressed.

"You sure you don't want to have some supper?" he asked her.

"I don't think it would be smart for us to be seen together," she said.

"Why's that?"

"We might be facing off against each other at town meetings in the future," she observed.

"You're still going to fight the opening of my place?" Clint asked.

"Did you think a little sex—or a lot of it—would change that?" she asked. "This town doesn't need a new saloon and gambling hall."

"I never thought about any sex being involved, at all," he pointed out. "Do you think I was trying to influence your thinking?"

"No, no," she said. "this was my idea—but a good one, don't you think?"

"I haven't decided on that, yet." He went to the door. "Stay as long as you like."

"I'm just going to give you a head start before I come down," she explained.

He nodded.

"I'll see you soon," she said.

As he left the room, he wondered if the next time they saw each other would be as friends or foes?

***

Clint had supper and ate it slowly, deep in thought about many things. For one, backing the marshal's play was risky. He didn't know how either man—Jackson or Holden—handled a gun. All he knew was what he had heard since coming to town. If it came to gunplay, he'd be learning about them first hand. That wasn't the way he preferred to do it.

And then there was Connie, who he felt needed some support. At the moment, she was living in fear, and she didn't deserve that.

But most of Clint's responsibility was to Rick Hartman and their partnership. He had to make sure the Gunsmith Saloon—the name was growing on him—opened with everything going for it. He had his manager, he had his crew working on the appearance, now he needed to find the girls, and the games.

After supper, he walked over to The Union, which had now become his saloon of choice in Laramie—until the Gunsmith Saloon opened.

***

Rex saw him as soon as he entered, even though The Union was crowded. He waved Clint over to the bar and had a beer waiting for him.

"How's it goin' over there?" Rex asked.

"Good," Clint said. "They're making a mess."

"Don't worry," Rex said. "It'll look great when those three are done. They're good carpenters. Meanwhile, I've got two girls hired."

"Already?"

"I have to tell you, they got very excited when they heard that The Gunsmith Saloon wasn't just a clever name. They wanna work for you."

That just about clinched it. The place was going to have to be called The Gunsmith Saloon.

"I'm glad to hear that," he said. "Where did you find them?"

"Don't tell anyone," Rex said, lowering his voice and leaning in, "but right here. They've already let the owner know they'll be leaving as soon as your place is ready. They just don't want the other girls to know."

"Are they here now?" Clint asked.

"Yeah, but I ain't gonna point them out to you," he said. "I told them they didn't have to audition for you, they were bein' hired by me."

"That's fair enough," Clint said.

"When the time comes," Rex promised, "I'll introduce them to you."

"I just wanted to talk some things over with you," Clint said.

"Like what?"

"Like gambling."

"I was thinking you'd want poker, since you have a certain reputation when it comes to cards," Rex said. "Then I was thinking faro, craps, a roulette wheel and maybe even a wheel of fortune."

"All sounds good."

"And can I make a suggestion about the name of the place?" Rex asked.

"Sure, go ahead."

"The Gunsmith Gambling Palace and Saloon," Rex said. "It says what the place is all about."

"I'll send that to Rick and see how he feels, but I like it."

"Do we need to get the word 'theater' into the name?" Rex asked.

"No," Clint said, "there's a stage, but we won't be doing theater. At least, not in the beginning."

"That suits me," Rex said. "I'd rather just run a nice, big, normal saloon."

"I can tell, from your suggestions," Clint said. "Your thinking goes right along with mine.

"I've got one more suggestion for you," Rex said. "Just one word."

"What's that?"

"Crystal."

Clint shook his head.

"I should put you in direct contact with Rick Hartman," he said. "He's thinking the same thing."

"There are already a couple of chandeliers there," Rex pointed out, "but we can bring in more, make the place really sparkle."

"Believe me, Rex," Clint said, "sparkle sounds real good to me."

Chapter Thirty

Clint's conversation with Rex impressed him, especially the part about not introducing him to the girls he had already hired. The man had a take charge attitude that Clint felt was important to do the job.

When he got back to his hotel, Abby was gone, but the smell of her lingered on his sheets. He didn't mind that, at all, and went to sleep thinking about her nipples...

***

When Clint came down the next morning, he found Marshal Jackson sitting in the lobby. The man seemed very nervous. Clint looked around, but there was nobody else in sight except the desk clerk.

"We were supposed to meet in your office," he said. "I was coming there after breakfast."

"You mind if we have breakfast together?" the lawman asked.

"No," Clint said, "but I was just going into the hotel dining room."

"That's fine with me."

They went into the dining room, were seated and ordered their breakfasts. Once they had coffee in front of them, Clint spoke.

"What's on your mind, Marshal?" he asked.

"Well . . . it's this thing about bracing Ben Holden," Jackson said.

"What about it?"

"Um . . . I don't wanna do it."

"You're the marshal."

Jackson took off the badge and set it down on the table.

"I don't wanna do that anymore, either."

"What the hell, Jackson," Clint said, "put the damn badge back on."

Jackson hesitated, then picked it up and pinned it back on.

"What's going on in your head?" Clint demanded.

"Ben Holden shootin' me, for one thing."

"How about me shooting you?" Clint asked. "Is that in your head?"

"You wouldn't shoot a lawman."

"Take the damn badge off again and I will shoot you," Clint said.

The waiter came with their breakfasts. They waited until he left to speak again.

"So you're a little nervous," Clint said. "That's why I'm going to back your play."

"See?" Jackson said. "'Back my play?' What's my play? You make it sound like I gotta use my gun. Do you know how many times I've even taken my gun outta my holster?"

"I wouldn't be surprised if the answer was never."

"It's not that, but hardly ever, and usually on drunks."

"Not on anybody who could shoot back?"

"No."

"How have you lived this long wearing a badge and not had to shoot anybody?"

"I told you," Jackson said, "drunks and dogs."

"Yeah," Clint said, "Well, this one time it might have to be different, but for a start we're just going to talk to Holden."

"When?"

"Right after breakfast," Clint said, "if we can find him."

***

It proved harder than they'd hoped.

The saloons weren't open yet, and Holden was not in any of the restaurants in town. Neither did they see him anywhere on the streets.

131

"You mean to tell me you have no idea where Holden lives?" Clint asked.

"None."

"And no one on the town council does, either?"

"As far as I know, that's true."

"Somebody must know," Clint said.

"But who?" Jackson asked.

"You'd know that better than I would," Clint said. "Talk to some people and see what you can find out."

"Where will you be?"

"Supervising the work on The Gunsmith Saloon."

***

Clint went to the site and entered midst all of the banging noises. He couldn't see anybody, but the noise certainly indicated a lot of work going on.

As he stepped further in, he looked up to the second level, saw Spencer working on reinforcing the railing there. The man saw him, stopped and waved.

"Hard at work, I see and hear," Clint said.

"Only way to go, Clint."

He heard banging from elsewhere in the building, assumed the other carpenters had the same attitude. It seemed he had hired the right men.

Chapter Thirty-One

Clint had to admit he didn't much care whether or not Marshal Jackson found Ben Holden. As far as he was concerned, if Holden left Connie alone, he was satisfied. And the mayor's murder was the concern of the lawman and the town council, not his.

He went to the bank to check in on Connie, who was seated at her desk. She smiled as he approached, no longer afraid to be seen with him.

"Are you all right?" he asked.

"Yes, I'm fine," she said. "I've been worrying about you."

"Don't," Clint said.

"But Holden—"

"I'm not going to have anything to do with Holden unless he bothers you," Clint said.

"That's good to hear," she said.

"Mr. Adams!"

Clint turned, saw the bank manager, Edward, coming toward him.

"So nice to see you," the man said. "How are things going at The Bucket of Blood?"

"We've decided that the new name will be The Gunsmith Saloon," Clint said.

"Excellent!" Edward said. "When will you be open-ing?"

"It won't be for some time," Clint said. "We're deep into renovations."

Edward seemed very happy with all the news.

"I look forward to the opening," he said. "Right now, I'm afraid I have to take Miss Rayland away from you."

"That's fine," Clint said. "I was just leaving."

As he did, Edward and Connie went into the manag-er's office.

***

After the bank, he went to the telegraph office to send Rick a progress report. He told his friend and partner that he had hired a manager, and a couple of girls, and that the renovations were well underway—with an eye toward crystal.

"You wanna wait for a reply?" the key operator asked.

"No," Clint said, "just bring it to my hotel." He gave the man four bits.

"Thank you, sir!"

Clint left the office, hoping Rick would be satisfied with the way things were going.

***

"Can you get him to do it?" Doug Cranford asked.

Marshal July Jackson was facing the five members of the town council.

"I think so," Jackson said, even though he wasn't all that sure he could get Clint Adams to kill Ben Holden.

"You think so?" Nola Ketchum barked. She was a longtime resident in her sixties, who owned several rooming houses and cafes in town. "We need to know, Marshal. If Holden killed the mayor, then he's got to go."

"Before anybody else steps up to take that office!" Bill Wolfson added, anxiously. "Ain't nobody gonna take that office if Holden's just gonna kill 'em." Wolfson had also lived in Laramie a long time. He owned three different livery stables in town.

"I can't make Adams kill 'im," Jackson pointed out. "But it seems to me them two going at it is just natural. It's gonna happen."

"You just need to help it along, Marshal," Jasper Ward said. Ward owned a big ranch just outside of town, was the most educated of the bunch, and the most likely to step into the mayor's office to take over.

The fifth member of the town council was Leo Hendry, who rarely, if ever, said a word. He simply voted with the majority, then went back to the mercantile store he owned, one of the largest businesses in town.

"What can we do to help it along?" Ward asked.

135

"Well," Jackson said, "if one of you was to hire Holden to go after Adams, that would do it. See, Holden's a gun for hire."

"You mean he won't do it unless he's paid?" Nola asked. "Shitfire, then let's pay 'im."

"Pay a man to get killed?" Cranford asked. "Is that what we're here for?"

"Do you wanna be mayor with Ben Holden still around?" Nola asked him.

"Nola, you know I don't want to be mayor at all," Cranford replied.

"One of you men oughtta step up," she said.

"What about you, Nola?" Cranford asked. "You think maybe Holden won't shoot a woman?"

Ward, ignoring both Cranford and Nola, said to the marshal, "You're saying Holden only kills when he's paid to. Who paid him to kill the mayor?"

The question hung in the air as the council members all turned their heads to look at each other.

Chapter Thirty-Two

As Marshal July Jackson left the town council meeting in City Hall, he knew he had to decide who he feared the most, Ben Holden or Clint Adams? He knew what Holden could do because he'd seen him. What he knew about Clint Adams was only what he had read and heard about the Gunsmith. In the end, the fact that Adams was a legend had to beat what he knew from personal experience.

So it was to Jackson's benefit if he told Clint Adams what the town council wanted him to do. When this was all over, Jackson didn't care whether or not he still wore the marshal's badge. It was becoming more and more clear to him that he wasn't cut out to be a lawman.

He was hoping to find out where Holden was before running into the Gunsmith again. But as he walked away from City Hall, Clint Adams was coming right towards him.

"You find him?" Clint asked.

"I ain't seen Holden at all," Jackson said, "Or heard where he might be."

"Well then, I can't help you until you do," Clint said. "I can't back a play that's not being made. When you find him, I'll be at the saloon."

"The Union?"

"No," Clint said, "The Gunsmith."

***

Clint sat in the saloon amidst the clatter. They had managed to locate some tables and chairs and set them up, to get an idea of what the arrangement might look like. Clint was sitting at one of those tables, trying to envision what the inside would and should look like when they were done.

Spencer came out of the back, saw Clint and walked over to join him.

"You want a drink?" he asked.

"What do you have?" Clint asked.

"We found some bottles of whiskey in the root cellar," Spencer said.

"I prefer beer."

"It's improved with age."

"That's okay," Clint said. "I'll have a beer at The Union in a little while."

"Later tonight," Spencer said, "we can all join you."

"Good." Clint rose. "I'll see you there."

"You don't have to leave," Spencer said.

"I don't feel right just sitting here while you and the others do all the work," Clint said. "I have to be doing something."

"Like finding Ben Holden?"

Clint had started for the door, but stopped short at that.

"What do you know about Holden?"

"The word's gone out that you're tryin' to find him."

"Since when?"

"Early today."

"How do you know?"

"Bannister had to go and pick some things up at the mercantile," Spencer said, "He came back with the news. Seems like you and Holden are headed for a showdown."

"Not of my making," Clint said. "I didn't put the word out."

"Then who did?"

"I think I may have an idea," Clint said.

***

Clint found Jackson in his office.

"You put the word out that I want Holden," Clint said.

"I had to do somethin'," the lawman said.

"Really? How about putting out the word that *you* want him?" Clint suggested.

139

"I—that wouldn't be—Adams, I'd be dead before I knew it," Jackson argued.

"So what do you expect to happen now?"

"Look," Jackson said, "I didn't tell you this before, but the town council wants you to kill Holden."

"Why?"

"They believe he killed the mayor," Jackson said. "They don't know why, so before someone steps up to take the mayor's place, they want to make sure they won't get shot."

"I thought Holden only killed who he was paid to kill?" Clint said.

"That's what we all thought," Jackson said. "Now we're wonderin' why he killed Mayor Long."

"Maybe," Clint said, "they had a falling out. It looked to me like Long may have tried to shoot Holden, maybe even in the back."

"Only Holden got him first," Jackson said.

"Yes."

"So if that's the case, he wouldn't kill another mayor."

"Not unless they tried to kill him, first," Clint said. "So Holden kills for hire, or for self-defense."

"And now . . ."

". . . and now he thinks I'm after him."

Chapter Thirty-Three

A face-to-face with Ben Holden seemed inevitable. Clint wasn't sure who to blame for that, the marshal or the entire town council. He wondered what Holden was planning. Make it happen, or avoid it? How confident was the man in his ability with a gun?

Clint decided to let the man come to him, if that's what he wanted to do. Perhaps they would even talk it out and not give the council what they wanted.

Jackson and Clint stepped out of the marshal's office together.

"Where are you goin' now?" Jackson asked.

"Back to The Gunsmith," Clint said.

"I better come along," Jackson said, "just in case."

"Just in case . . . what? Holden finds me, or you?" Clint asked.

"I was just—"

"Never mind," Clint said. "If you want to come with me, come ahead."

***

Things hadn't changed in the short time since he'd been there last. There was still banging going on from downstairs and upstairs and—if Clint's hearing was accurate—from the roof. There was also a lot of dust floating about.

"Jesus," Jackson said, fanning the air with his hand, "this smells like old dust."

"It probably is," Clint said. "This place was closed up for a long time." Jackson coughed. "You don't have to stay, you know."

"It looks like it's settlin' down," Jackson said.

"Let's go sit over there," Clint said, pointing. "It looks cleaner."

They walked to a table that had some chairs upside down on it. They righted two of the chairs and sat.

"Anythin' to drink?" Jackson asked.

"There's some whiskey, somewhere," Clint said. "Probably as old as the dust."

"It gets better with age," Jackson said.

"So I've heard," Clint said. "I prefer beer, myself."

"Beer goes bad."

"Yes, it does," Clint said.

Some of the hammering stopped and moments later Spencer came down the stairs.

"Hey," he said. "Checkin' up on us?"

"Not on you," Clint said, "just on the progress."

"Well, the roof's patched," Spencer said. "We'll know more when it rains."

"So what's next?" Clint asked.

"A couple of the upstairs rooms need new windows. I'm gonna get right on that, but first . . . you guys want a drink?"

"You fellas cracked a bottle?" Clint asked.

"No," Stark said, coming down the stairs, covered with dust. "We figured we'd wait for you."

"Where's Bannister?" Clint asked.

"In the back, working on some sections we're gonna use to fortify the upstairs railing."

Clint looked at Jackson, who wiped his hand across his mouth.

"Yeah, okay," Clint said, "open a bottle and we'll have one each."

"I'll get it," Stark said. "And Bannister."

He went into the back room, returned in seconds with Bannister and a bottle of whiskey.

"No glasses," he said. "We'll have to pass the bottle around."

"One drink each," Clint repeated. "After the workday, we can all go to The Union for real drinks."

They all agreed.

"You know," Marshal Jackson said, "The Union is the most likely place for us to run into Ben Holden."

"Well, we wanted to do it more privately, but I guess we'll have to take what we can get."

"You and Holden?" Bannister said, passing the bottle to Stark. "That oughtta be somethin' to see."

"Why are you after Holden?" Spencer asked, accepting the bottle from Stark.

"The Marshal, here, and the town council believe that Holden killed the mayor."

"Yeah, we heard about that," Stark said. "That's too bad. Didn't the mayor have a connection to this place?"

Bannister nodded. "His family owned it for a long time. You came here after they was hung."

"So who's gonna be mayor now?" Spencer asked, passing the bottle to Clint.

"Nobody wants the job," Clint said, "unless they're convinced they aren't going to be killed."

"Why would Holden wanna kill the mayor?" Bannister asked.

Clint, after a very small sip of whiskey, passed the bottle to Jackson, who took a large swig.

"That's what we're going to find out," Clint said.

Chapter Thirty-Four

Before Clint left the saloon, his new manager, Rex, made an appearance. By then they had tucked the bottle of whiskey away in the back room, again.

"We were just coming over to The Union," Clint said.

"We?"

"Me and the marshal," Clint said. "The rest of these fellas later on."

"I just thought I'd stop in for a look," Rex said. "I can walk back with ya."

"You know," Clint said, "I hired you as manager without even finding out your last name."

"Donovan," the bartender said. "Rex Donovan."

"Okay," Clint said. "I'll pass your full name over to my partner. Next week we'll start paying you."

"You know," Rex said, "as long as I'm still workin' at The Union, you don't have to pay me until this place actually opens. I'd feel like I was takin' money for nothin'."

"I tell you what," Clint said, "you've already hired some girls, and you're working on the gaming. We'll pay you half your salary until the place opens."

"Okay," Rex said, "I'll go along with that."

Clint told Rex some of what was going on in the building, and then they headed for the door to walk over to The Union, with the marshal.

"Is, uh, Holden at The Union?" Jackson asked.

"What?" Rex asked.

"Ben Holden," Jackson said. "Is he over there?"

"No," Rex said. "I ain't seen 'im . . . yet. He should be comin' in, though. Oh yeah, I heard you guys were lookin' for him." He looked at Clint. "You ain't gonna shoot up The Union, are ya?"

"That's not my plan," Clint said.

"Good," Rex said, "because sooner or later you fellas are gonna run into each other there. I'd just appreciate it if you took it outside."

"Let's see if he shows up," Clint said, "and then we can take it from there."

The three men walked over to The Union together. Rex reclaimed his place behind the bar and served Clint and Jackson a beer each.

"I don't see 'im," Jackson said, looking around.

"Relax, Marshal," Clint said. "Just enjoy your beer."

"I can't help bein' nervous," Jackson said.

"Maybe he's nervous, too," Clint suggested. "Maybe he won't come in."

"You think so?" Jackson said. "I thought men like you and him didn't get nervous."

"Me and him?" Clint asked.

"You know," Jackson said. "Killers."

"Killers?"

"Well . . . come on," Jackson said. "No offense, I'm just talkin' about your reputation."

"Yeah," Clint said, "sure."

"Look, Adams—" Jackson said.

"Forget it, Marshal," Clint said, pushing the rest of his beer away. "I'm tired of waiting here. If he comes in, you talk to him."

"B-but . . ." Jackson stammered, ". . . you were gonna back my play."

"Really?" Clint asked. "You want a killer backing you?"

He left before Jackson could respond.

***

Ben Holden didn't like the idea of Clint Adams looking for him. He wanted it to be the other way around. The word was also out that the marshal was looking for him, but he wasn't worried about July Jackson. Only the Gunsmith. He was going to need an edge, and he thought he knew what it could be.

Nobody in town knew where Holden lived, and he kept it that way. He left the abandoned building he used and headed into town.

***

Clint didn't feel like returning to his hotel, or going to another saloon, so he just headed back to The Gunsmith. Even if Stark, Spencer and Bannister had left, he could sit there alone and do some thinking.

He was about to cross the street from the hat shop to the saloon when the door opened, and Abby Wells appeared.

"Where are you headed?" she asked, stepping out.

"Across the street."

"I saw your carpenters leave a little while ago," she said. "There's nobody over there."

"That's okay with me," he said. "I could use the time alone."

"Really?" she asked. "I'm headed home now, and I've got some cold fried chicken there. Maybe that'd interest you?"

"Maybe it would," Clint said.

She linked her arm into his.

"Then maybe we can see what happens next."

Chapter Thirty-Five

The fried chicken was very tasty. What came after was absolutely delectable.

Abby's long, lean body responded to the slightest touch of Clint's hand and mouth. Her large nipples blossomed even before he touched them directly, and then when he did, she gasped and arched her back.

When he slid his hand down between her legs and slid a finger into her, she gushed, wetting his hand and the sheet beneath her.

"Oh God," she said, trembling, "no man's ever made me do that before."

"Then no man's ever touched you in the right way," he pointed out.

"You got *that* right," she breathed.

He continued to stroke her pussy and suck on her nipples until her trembling seemed to shake the room, then mounted her and drove his hard cock into her wet, steamy depths.

"Ah, Jesus!" she cried out, wrapping those long legs around him. "Oh yes!"

Clint usually favored full bodied women, but this slender creature's responses were captivating.

Clint drove himself in and out of her, urged on by not only her words but her reactions, until he exploded inside her with loud roar . . .

***

In another part of town, when the knock came at her door, Connie Rayland felt sure it was Clint Adams. She swung the door open with a smile on her face, but it disappeared when she saw Ben Holden standing there.

"Hello, little lady," he said.

"You said you wouldn't bother me again," she responded.

"I know," he said, "but somethin's come up, and I need you to come with me again."

"You can't—"

He raised a hand to cut her off and said, "This time I'm askin', ain't I? I'm not just grabbin' you off the street."

"It's still kidnapping," she told him.

"Naw, it ain't, at all," he said. "I just need you to spend a little time with me, is all. Hey, I'll even feed you real good. Now, just get yourself ready and come along." He stepped inside and closed the door behind him with a smile. "I'll wait here."

***

Later, Clint was on his back with Abby roaming his body with her hands and mouth, returning the favor. He closed his eyes as she took his penis into her mouth and began to suck it. Her head bobbed up and down as she wet it with her tongue, top to bottom, and then began to suck faster and faster, moaning as she did.

Clint started his own groaning as he reached down to cup her head with both hands. This lady may not have been having sex very much, lately—according to her— but she sure as hell knew what she was doing.

He tried to hold back as long as he could, but that mouth of hers just wouldn't have it, and before long he exploded . . .

***

"So?" she asked, moments later.

"So what?" he asked, still trying to catch his breath.

She rolled over, pressed her naked body to his and asked, "How was the chicken?"

"That was some of the best chicken I ever tasted," he replied.

"You should've tasted it when it was hot," she said. "Maybe, one night, before you leave town, I'll cook you a hot supper."

"That'd be great," he said.

"And then," she added, sliding her hand up and down his thigh, "we could see what else happens."

***

"Where are we going?" Connie asked Ben Holden.

They were walking through some of the lesser traveled streets of Laramie, with darkness falling.

"You found your way home from here the last time," Holden said. "You will, again."

"You're not blindfolding me?" she asked.

"There's no need."

"D-does that mean you're gonna k-kill me?" she asked.

"No," Holden said, "I'm not gonna kill you, girl. I'm gonna let you go, as soon as I do what I have to do."

"Which is?" she asked.

"There are a lot of people in town who want Clint Adams to kill me," Holden said. "So I'm gonna kill him, first, and you're gonna help me."

Chapter Thirty-Six

When Clint got back to his hotel, he was surprised to see Ben Holden sitting on the porch. A nearby torch illuminated the gunman's face as he stood and smiled.

"We need to talk," he said.

"I guess we do," Clint said. "Right here good?"

"It's fine," Holden said. "I'd rather do it here than in your room, or in a saloon."

"Then let's sit," Clint said.

They each took a chair and sat side-by-side, rather than facing each other.

"First of all," Clint said, "if you've heard that I'm looking for you to kill you, you've heard wrong."

"That's what I heard."

"The marshal is actually looking for you to have a talk," Clint said.

"Only he put it out there that it was you," Holden said.

"Right."

"Well," Holden said, "what I'm hearin' is that there are folks hereabouts who want you to kill me."

"I don't kill people just because somebody wants me to," Clint said. "And from what I've heard about you, you don't do it unless you're being paid."

"That's true," Holden said, "usually."

"The word around town is you broke that rule when you killed Mayor Long."

"Who says I killed the mayor?" Holden asked.

"Everybody," Clint said. "The town council, the marshal, people on the street."

Holden leaned back in his chair.

"Is there any point to me denyin' it?"

"There is," Clint said, "if you didn't do it."

"Does it really make a difference?" Holden asked. "Whether I did it or not, you and me are gonna have a showdown, ain't we?"

"That's going to be up to you," Clint said.

"I suppose it is," Holden said. "What about Marshal Jackson? Am I gonna have to kill him, too?"

"I don't think the marshal has the gumption to face you, Holden."

"So then it's just gonna be you and me," Holden said.

"Look," Clint said, "I came here to buy a saloon. For me to do anything else, I'm going to have to be pushed."

"Well," Holden said, standing up, "when the time comes, I'll probably push ya."

"If I was you, I wouldn't," Clint said.

"I gotta tell ya, I wouldn't do it unless I had an edge."

"And do you have one?"

"I do."

"What is it?"

"I can't tell you that right now," Holden said, "but tomorrow you'll find out."

"And how will I do that?" Clint asked.

"Just durin' the course of your day," Holden said. "Once you know what it is, we'll talk again."

"Holden—" Clint started, but the man stepped down from the porch and walked off into the darkness.

Clint sat there alone for a few minutes, going over the conversation in his head. He thought he knew what edge Holden was referring to and didn't like the idea of waiting until the next day to find out, so he quickly got to his feet and left the porch.

***

He banged on Connie Rayland's door again and again, despite being fairly confident that she wasn't inside. Holden had taken her somewhere and was going to use her against Clint.

He peered in the windows, toyed with the idea of forcing the door, but in the end decided it was useless. Ben Holden had her.

He headed for the marshal's office.

***

July Jackson looked up in surprise, and then fear, which was what Clint wanted.

"What the—" Jackson started, but Clint cut him off.

"Jackson, you're going to stop being a worthless piece of shit of a lawman," Clint snapped.

"W-what's goin' on?" Jackson asked. "Did you find Ben Holden?"

"He found me," Clint said. "He was waiting for me at my hotel."

"Did you kill 'im?" Jackson looked hopeful, which made Clint even madder.

"No, I didn't kill him," Clint said. "He came to tell me he had an edge over me."

"An edge?" Jackson said. "What edge?"

"Constance Rayland."

"The bank lady? I thought she was all right?"

"She was," Clint said, "but I'm sure he's grabbed her again, and this time he intends to use her against me."

"Are—are you gonna let 'im do that?"

"What the hell choice do I have?" Clint demanded.

"So you're gonna let him kill you instead of the girl?" Jackson asked, confused.

"I'm not going to let him kill anybody," Clint said. "Just listen closely . . ."

***

Clint forced himself to go back to his hotel for a good night's sleep. He felt sure Ben Holden would appear sometime the next day, looking to put his "edge" into play.

Chapter Thirty-Seven

The next morning Clint dressed and went down for breakfast. He wanted to leave himself out in the public eye for Holden to find, so he left the hotel and walked to a nearby café. It was busy, but he managed to do something he normally never did. He got himself a table in the window. He doubted Holden would take a shot at him through the glass, but he wanted the man to see him. It was probably one of the meals he had enjoyed the least in his entire life. Sitting in the window was just not relaxing, at all.

He ate his breakfast quickly, keeping an alert eye out the window. By the time he was finished, he had never seen Ben Holden on the street.

He left the café, looked the street over carefully, then started walking. His intention was to do so aimlessly, but before long he found himself in front of The Gunsmith Saloon, with sounds of work emanating from inside.

He went through the door.

***

Connie Rayland was once again tied to a chair, but this time Holden did not gag her.

"Nobody would hear you, anyway," he said, as he entered the abandoned building he called home. He had a tray of food in his hands, breakfast for both of them. He put it down on a rickety table and untied her hands.

"I thought we'd eat together," he told her. "Nice and friendly-like."

She wanted to tell him she wasn't hungry, but it wasn't true. She was starving. She turned her chair so she could face the table, her feet still tied. There was nothing to do but eat.

Both plates were covered with bacon-and-eggs, so she simply grabbed one and dug in.

"See?" Holden said. "I told you I'd feed you good."

"How long is this going to take?" she asked. "How long do I have to be here?"

"That'll depend on Adams," Holden said.

"I don't understand," she said, "what Clint ever did to you."

"Nothin'," Holden said. "It's not what he did, it's what he's gonna do."

"And what's that?" she asked. "Open a new saloon?"

"I don't care about that," Holden said. "He might not be plannin' to, but he's gonna try to kill me. So I gotta kill him first."

"Why don't you just leave town?" she asked.

"I ain't gonna run."

"Then just hide until he leaves town," she suggested.

"I ain't gonna hide, neither," he said.

"So just get it over with."

"I am," he said. "And you're gonna help me."

"How can I help you kill a man?" she asked. "I'm a bank clerk."

Holden smiled.

"You're just gonna give me an edge," he explained. "Keep eatin'."

***

Clint spent the morning in The Gunsmith Saloon, talking with the carpenters, watching them work, even pitching in when another set of hands was needed.

He had stopped by Connie's place first, but she still wasn't there. He had also checked the bank, but they hadn't seen her. The manager, Edward, was worried, and asked Clint to let him know when he found out anything.

He could have spent his time looking for Connie, but there was no point. Holden wasn't going to hurt her as long as he could use her for his "edge." So all Clint had to do was wait for the gunman to bring her out into the open.

Until then he needed to occupy himself, and the saloon was as good a place as any.

***

July Jackson stood at the window of his office, staring out at the street. He wasn't exactly disappointed with the Gunsmith's new plan for handling Ben Holden. He pretty much told the lawman to stay off the streets, and out of the way.

"Whether or not you want to keep being a lawman when this is all over is up to you," the Gunsmith told him. "You took the badge off once, and my advice would be to take it off again. But don't do anything Ben Holden has to deal with."

"So you are gonna kill him?" Jackson asked.

"I'm going to do what's necessary to get him to leave Connie Rayland alone," Clint explained. "That poor girl hasn't done anything to deserve this, except sell me a saloon."

Jackson didn't know if he would keep the badge or not, but he could wait for Holden to be gone, and a new mayor to be sworn in, before making up his mind.

For now, he was going to do just what the Gunsmith told him to do.

Stay out of the way.

Chapter Thirty-Eight

Clint sat in The Union later in the day with Spencer, Stark and Bannister. They all had beers in front of them.

"If you're lookin' for work," Bannister said to him, "I'd hire ya."

"Yeah, you got good hands," Stark said. "If I wasn't workin' for you, I'd hire you to work for me."

"That's okay," Clint said. "I was just killing some time."

"Until what?" Spencer asked.

Clint didn't answer right away, so Bannister said, "Until he has to kill a man."

"What do you know about it?" Clint asked.

"I know if you're gonna be involved with Ben Holden, one of you is gonna end up dead. Right now, I'd rather it be him, since you're payin' me and he ain't."

"I gotta get some sleep," Spencer said.

"Me, too," Stark agreed.

They both stood up and said good-night. That left Clint and Bannister alone. There was a lot of activity going on around them, but nobody could hear them.

"What was that about?"

"Ben Holden," Bannister said. "None of us wanna see you get killed, Clint."

"Neither do I," Clint said. "Why did that mean they had to leave us alone?"

"I've lived here longer than either of them," Bannister said. "They don't know Ben Holden real well."

"And you do?"

"Better than them," Bannister said, "and better than most."

"Meaning?"

Bannister leaned in.

"Meaning I can tell you where he lives."

This time Clint leaned in.

***

After breakfast Holden left Connie tied to the chair and left. He had decided to let the Gunsmith wait a bit longer, let it play on his mind exactly what Holden's edge might be. And even if he figured it out and realized the girl was gone, it would eat at him, increasing Holden's edge.

Holden had lived in Laramie for some time, but once he had killed the Gunsmith, he would be too big for one town.

Later in the day, Holden put in an appearance at The Union Saloon, thinking the Gunsmith would be there. He got a beer at the bar and waited, knowing the Gunsmith wouldn't touch him until he knew what Holden's edge was.

***

Clint followed Bannister's directions to the abandoned house he said Holden was living in. If he was holding Connie, he would probably be there.

He approached quietly. The house was dilapidated, with shutters hanging from the windows, the porch rail broken, some roof tiles on the ground at the base of the house. He stepped up onto the porch, careful not to walk where the boards were broken so he wouldn't snap his ankle. About the only benefit he could see for Holden to live there was that it was rent free, and nobody would look for him there.

Clint peered in the dirty windows, and saw Connie tied to a chair in the center of the room. He decided to just walk through the front door, and if Holden was there, they'd get it over with.

As he entered, Connie's head jerked up. It was dusk, and the interior of the house was dark, but he could see the surprise in her eyes.

"Clint!"

"Is he here?" Clint asked.

She shook her head.

"No, he's not."

He rushed to her side and untied her. She leaned against him for a moment, and then he helped her stand.

"Are you all right? Can you walk?"

"Yes, I'm fine," she said. "He didn't hurt me. Apparently, he just wanted to use me against you. How did you find me?"

"A friend told me where Holden lived," Clint said. "I figured he'd be holding you here."

"What do we do now?" she asked.

"Well, we get out of this shack before it falls down."

"That suits me."

They both stepped outside, carefully navigating the porch, until they were on firm ground.

"Holden thinks he has an edge over me," Clint said, "because he figures he has you. I'm going to let him keep thinking that until he comes back here later and sees that you're gone. Meanwhile, don't go home. Is there someone you can stay with?"

"Yes," she said, "Helen, a woman at the bank. She'll let me stay with her until . . . until when?"

"Until this is all over, Connie," Clint said.

"And when will that be?"

"Sooner than Holden thinks," he said.

Chapter Thirty-Nine

Clint walked Connie to Helen's house, where the older woman welcomed her warmly.

"You leave her here, Mr. Adams, and do what you must," Helen said. "She'll be safe with me."

"Clint," Connie said, "please be careful."

"I will," Clint said. "I'll see you later, or tomorrow."

From Helen's house he went to The Union, figuring he would start looking for Holden there. When he entered, he saw that he had made the right decision. Holden was standing at the bar with a beer, and, when he saw Clint, he raised it in an arrogant salute.

Clint approached the bar and the patrons gathered there, sensing something was about to happen, spread out to make room.

"Buy you a beer?" Holden asked.

"I think I should buy you one," Clint said. "I'm celebrating."

"Oh?" Holden said. And what would you have to celebrate?"

"I've managed to dull your edge," Clint said, "considerably."

"What?" Holden put his half-finished beer down on the bar. "What are you talkin' about?"

"Why don't you go home and find out," Clint said. "But first, let's get you a fresh one."

"Go to hell!" Holden shouted, and stormed out of the saloon.

Rex brought Clint a beer and said, "He's not happy."

"He's going to be even less happy when he gets home," Clint said.

"He has a home?" Rex asked.

"It's not much," Clint said, picking up his beer, "but he calls it home."

Rex leaned his elbows on the bar.

"Is this thing between you two comin' to a head?"

"It should be."

"Well, for my sake," he said, "I hope you come out of it okay."

"Don't worry," Clint said, "even if he kills me, you'll have a job."

"Hey, I didn't me—" Rex said, standing straight, realizing he may have insulted Clint.

"It's okay," Clint said. "Don't worry about it."

But Rex, still flustered, said, "Uh, I gotta get back to work."

Clint let him go.

***

167

Ben Holden charged into his house, saw the empty chair and kicked it across the room. He didn't know who had told the Gunsmith where he lived, but only a few people knew. He took off his hat, ran his hand through his hair, trying to calm himself down. He thought he had Clint Adams right where he wanted him, but now they were on equal terms. All he had to do was convince himself that he was faster than the Gunsmith. Adams was older than he was, and as far as gunplay, had been at it longer. He had to be slowing down. Holden knew he was getting faster every day.

He righted the chair and sat on it. He could go back to The Union right now and face Adams, but he still wanted to make the man wait. Let him wonder when it was coming.

***

July Jackson left his office.

He had come to a decision. If he gave up his badge and left Laramie, what would he do? Where would he go? Trail drives were a thing of the past, and he couldn't see himself working as a clerk in a mercantile.

It was actually taking the badge off, letting it sit in his hand while he studied it, that made up his mind for him.

He put the badge back on, tapped it, and left, heading for The Union Saloon. He hoped he wasn't too late.

***

Clint was surprised when July Jackson walked into the saloon. The lawman spotted him and came walking over.

"I know, I know," Jackson said, before Clint could speak. "You told me to stay out of it, but I can't. I'm the law, until somebody tells me otherwise."

"Like a new mayor?" Clint asked.

"I have no idea who that's gonna be," Jackson said, "so I might as well just do my job until I find out." He looked around. "Where's Holden?"

"He was here, but after I told him he'd lost his edge, he stormed out."

"Think he'll be back tonight?" Jackson asked.

"I doubt it," Clint said. "He needs time to think. How about a beer?"

"I was hopin' you'd say that," Marshal Jackson said.

Chapter Forty

The next morning Clint was at the saloon when Bannister arrived for work.

"I thought I'd see you at The Union, last night," he said to the big man.

"Naw," Bannister said. "I didn't want to be around if things came to a head with you and Holden."

"It didn't," Clint said, "but I did manage to get the girl away from him, thanks to you."

"Just don't tell him how you found where he lives," Bannister said.

"Don't worry," Clint said. "That's just between you and me."

"Good," the big man said. "Let's keep it that way."

He entered the saloon carrying a large tool box. Clint turned, saw Stark and Spencer crossing the street toward him.

"Come to get your hands dirty again?" Stark asked.

"Not today," Clint said. "I've got to keep my hands free."

"That's what we heard," Spencer said. "Don't get yourself killed."

"I'll do my best."

The two carpenters went inside.

Clint decided to go back to his hotel, sit on the porch and wait for Ben Holden to make up his mind.

***

"I thought you'd be here," Marshal July Jackson said.

"What else is there to do?" Clint asked.

"I thought you might go after Holden."

"That would mean I was pushing for a fight," Clint said. "No matter what you think, I don't kill a man unless he makes me. Gives me no other choice."

"You think Holden's gonna do that?"

"I think he's trying to make up his mind," Clint said. "But I'm ready for it, either way. If he wants to walk away and forget the whole thing, I'm all for it."

"From what I know about Holden," Jackson said, "that just ain't gonna happen."

"Like I said," Clint replied, "either way."

"You mind if I sit here with ya, and wait? I got nothin' else to do," Jackson said.

"Be my guest," Clint said.

***

Holden saw Clint Adams and Marshal July Jackson sitting on the porch of the Laramie Valley Hotel.

He didn't see Jackson as a threat. In fact, he expected the lawman to hide in his office until Holden's business with Clint Adams was taken care of. Seeing him sitting there with the Gunsmith was a surprise. But maybe the lawman felt safer staying close to Adams. In any case, Holden was looking to kill the Gunsmith, not a lawman. Killing the Gunsmith would make him a big man. Killing a marshal would make him a wanted man.

He decided to approach them head on and see what they were planning.

He stepped up onto the porch and stared at the two men.

"I'm guessing," Clint said, speaking first, "that it was the mayor who had you grab the girl, and probably wanted you to kill me, but then he changed his mind and you killed him. Am I close?"

When Holden didn't answer, Jackson asked Clint, "Why would the mayor want you dead?"

"I guess only Holden knows," Clint said. "Or maybe he doesn't." Clint looked at Holden. "When somebody hires you to kill a person, do you have to know why to do the job?"

Holden hesitated, then said, "Naw, I don't need no reason. I just need to know how much."

"How much did the mayor pay you?" Clint asked.

"He didn't pay me."

"But how much was he *going* to pay you?"

"I never said he was gonna pay me," Holden pointed out.

"No, you didn't."

"So this is how things are gonna work now?" Holden asked. "You two are gonna watch each other's backs?"

"We're just sitting here," Clint said. "What did you have in mind?"

Holden addressed Jackson directly.

"I have nothin' against you, Marshal," Holden said. "I wouldn't be stupid enough to kill a lawman."

"Just stupid enough to go up against the Gunsmith," Jackson replied.

"We'll have to see," Holden said, "won't we?"

He turned and stepped down from the porch and walked away.

"I don't get it," Jackson said. "Why would Mayor Long have paid him to kill you?"

"We'll probably never know that," Clint said. "It could have had something to do with me buying the saloon his family once owned,"

"Gettin' that place up and runnin' can only be good for this town," Jackson said.

"Maybe that's why the mayor tried to call him off," Clint suggested. "Holden might have simply decided to take the matter into his own hands."

"The matter?"

"He decided it would be to his own benefit to kill me," Clint explained. "He finally found a job he didn't need to be paid to do."

Chapter Forty-One

It didn't take long for Ben Holden to figure out who told the Gunsmith where he lived. There were three suspects in town, and Clint Adams had a connection to only one of them.

As he entered the new Gunsmith Saloon—there was no sign out front, yet, but word had gotten around—he heard the hammering from different parts of the building. Knowing that Bannister was a big man with a lot of weight, he figured he would be on the first floor. The banging was coming from the back room, so he crossed the casino floor.

As he entered the back room, he saw Lance Bannister's broad back as the man was bent over a piece of furniture. He waited for the hammering to stop so the man could hear him.

"Pretty busy, huh, Bannister?" he asked.

Bannister straightened and looked behind him with a frown. Judging by the look on his face, he wasn't happy with what he saw.

"Holden," he said. "What brings you here? Lookin' for Adams?"

"No, Bannister," he said, "I'm lookin' for you."

Bannister straightened, still holding a hammer in his big hand.

"What can I do for you?" Bannister asked.

"Adams found out where I lived," Holden said. "That could only have come from you."

Bannister looked down at the hammer.

"What are ya gonna do?" he asked. "Shoot me? I'm unarmed."

"I'm a gunman, Lance," Holden said. "If I'm wearin' a gun, I'm armed. You're a carpenter. If you're carryin' a hammer, you're armed."

"You're kiddin'," Bannister said.

"I ain't," Holden said. "Make your play."

"Now hold on—"

"Do it now, Bannister!"

All Bannister could do was throw the hammer and hope for the best . . .

***

Spencer and Stark were both on the second floor, and as fate would have it, they stopped hammering in time to hear the shot from downstairs.

"What the hell was that?" Stark asked, coming out into the hall where Spencer was.

"Sounds like it came from downstairs."

Both men ran to the stairs and down to the first floor.

"Lance?" Stark called.

"Bannister!" Spencer yelled.

They both ran to the back room. When they got there, they found Bannister on the floor next to the piece of furniture he had been working on. There was a bullet in his chest and his sightless eyes were staring straight up at the ceiling. They looked around and found his hammer across the room, as if he had thrown it.

"Jesus," Stark swore, "who'd wanna kill Lance?"

"We better tell Clint," Spencer said. "Maybe he can figure it out."

"I'll find 'im," Stark said. "One of us better stay here."

"I guess," Spencer said, looking down at the big man. "Poor Lance."

"I'll be back," Stark said, and ran from the room. Spencer continued to stare down at his deceased friend.

***

Clint saw Stark running toward the hotel and knew something was wrong.

"Uh-oh," he said, standing up.

"What?" Jackson asked.

"I think we've got trouble."

They walked to the edge of the porch to meet Stark.

"What's wrong?" Clint asked.

"It's Bannister," Stark said, breathless. "Somebody shot 'im."

"How is he?" Clint asked.

"He's dead, Clint."

"Damn!" Clint immediately thought of Holden. If the gunman had figured out that it was the big carpenter who told Clint where he lived, it made sense that he'd kill him.

"We better get over there," Jackson said.

"I'll go with Stark," Clint said. "You get the undertaker."

"Right."

"And some men to move the body."

"Gotcha," Jackson said.

Clint started walking with Stark.

"What happened?"

"Spencer and me were upstairs, and we heard the shot. We came runnin' down and found him. That's all we know."

"That's okay," Clint said. "I have a good idea who killed him."

"You talkin' about Holden?"

Clint nodded.

"But why?"

"Bannister told me where Holden lived," Clint said. "Holden must've figured that out."

"Would he kill 'im, for that?"

"To try to get inside my head, yeah," Clint said. He knew Holden was still looking for that edge.

Chapter Forty-Two

Clint looked down sadly at the dead Lance Bannister.

"His hammer's across the room," Spencer said. "Looks like he threw it."

"He must've thought that was the only chance he had," Clint said.

"So who could've done it?" Spencer asked.

"It had to be Holden," Clint said.

"Lance told Clint where Holden lives," Stark said.

"I didn't know he knew," Spencer said.

"He knew," Clint said. "I guess he should've kept it to himself."

The marshal arrived with a dark suited man in tow, the undertaker.

"Oh my," the undertaker said, looking down at Bannister. "He's a big man." The undertaker himself was a rather small man in his fifties.

"I want the best box you've got," Clint said, "and treat him with respect."

"Of course, sir." He took out a handkerchief, wiped his sweaty face, and returned it to his pocket.

"I've got half a dozen men comin' to carry him," Jackson said.

"Good."

"You thinkin' it was Holden?" Jackson asked.

"Couldn't have been anybody else."

"So what now?" the marshal asked.

"I told you I only kill when I'm forced to," Clint said. "Well, now I've been forced."

***

Clint told the other two carpenters they could stop working for the day if they wanted to, but they both said they would keep at it.

Clint and Marshal Jackson stayed with the body until the men arrived to carry it off.

"You better go with them, Marshal," Clint said.

"You don't want me to stay with you and back your play?" Jackson asked.

"I don't want you to stay with me and get killed," Clint said, "or get me killed. Sorry, but that's the way it is."

"I get it," Jackson said. "I wish you luck against Holden."

"I'll take it," Clint said. "I might need it."

***

When Clint came out of The Gunsmith Saloon, there was a crowd just across the street, in front of Abby Wells' shop. Abby, herself, was standing there, arms folded, looking worried. She seemed relieved when he crossed the street toward her.

"I saw Holden—" she started, but Clint cut her short.

"Not here," he said. "Let's go inside."

Inside her shop, he told her not to talk to anybody else.

"Not the marshal?" she asked.

"Nobody!" Clint said, grabbing her by the shoulders. "If Holden hears that you saw him, he'll come after you."

"I'm not afraid of him!" she said, indignantly.

"Well, I am," he said. "And you should be. Look, I'll take care of Holden. Just don't talk to anybody."

"All right," she agreed.

"Now tell me exactly what you saw," he said.

"I heard a shot, and when I looked out the window, I saw him come out," she said.

"Was he running?" Clint asked.

"Not at all," she said. "He just sort of . . . sauntered off. What happened?"

"He killed one of my carpenters."

"Well, I was afraid he had killed you," she admitted.

"He didn't," Clint said. "But he'll get his chance."

"Why?" she asked. "Why would you give him a chance?"

"Because the alternative would be to shoot him in the back," Clint explained, "and I don't hold with that. I never have."

"Not even to save your life?"

"What kind of life would I have if I was a backshooter?" he asked. "I wouldn't be able to live with myself."

"I guess I'd have a hard time being a man, then," she said, "because I'd do anything I had to do to stay alive."

"Abby," Clint said, "I, for one, am very happy that you're not a man."

"You know," she said, giving him a look, "I could just pull the shades down—"

"Not right now," he said. "I'm afraid I've got something else on my mind."

"But why not stay here with me and let the marshal handle it?" she asked.

"Because he can't," Clint said. "And he'd just get himself killed."

"So it all falls to you?"

"Now that he's killed a friend of mine," Clint said, heading for the door, "I'm afraid it does."

Chapter Forty-Three

Clint checked Ben Holden's dilapidated house, but the man wasn't there. He then checked on Connie at Helen's house, and found that she was all right. He told her about the shooting, so she wouldn't hear the news and assume the worst.

He went to the undertaker's office and found the marshal there with the town doctor.

"We needed Doc Phillips to pronounce him dead," Jackson explained.

The white-haired sawbones said, "He was shot right through the heart, died instantly."

"Okay, Doc, thanks," Marshal Jackson said.

The doctor left.

"Would you like to view the deceased, sir?" the undertaker asked Clint.

"No, thanks," Clint said, "I did that already."

Clint and Jackson left the office and stopped just outside.

"I have to arrest Holden," Jackson said, unhappily.

"For what?" Clint asked. "What can you prove?"

"Well . . . nothin', I guess."

"Then stay out of it," Clint said. "Now it really is just between him and me. I know I've been going back and forth on this, but now I have no choice. You can't prove he killed Bannister, and you can't prove he killed the mayor."

"Neither can you."

"I don't have to have proof," Clint said. "I'm not the law. I know he did it, and I'm going to make him pay."

"What about your saloon?"

"Stark and Spencer will continue to work on it," Clint said. "I'm going to have them hire more men so things go faster. But once they're done, I don't know if I want anything to do with it, anymore. I'll have to talk to my partner about that."

"So you won't call it The Gunsmith Saloon?"

"I haven't made up my mind, yet."

"Well," Jackson said, "I've got to tell the council what's goin' on. They're gonna ask."

"Just tell them you've got everything under control," Clint said.

"You think they're gonna believe that?" Jackson asked.

"Make them believe it," Clint said. "You're the law, remember?"

***

Clint's next stop was The Union, which was doing a light business in the afternoon.

Rex had a beer on the bar by the time Clint reached it.

"It's early," Clint said, "but I need this."

"I heard there was a shootin' at your place this mornin'," Rex said. "I thought it might be you killin' Holden, or him killin' you."

"Lance Bannister's dead," Clint said.

"What?"

"It looks like Holden shot him."

"Sonofabitch!" Rex said. "Bannister was a good man."

"Yes, he was."

"What are you gonna do?" Rex asked.

"Get revenge for him."

"Kill Holden?"

"I'll kill him, or he'll kill me," Clint said. "One way or another, it'll be over."

"Are you sure?"

"I've been trying to avoid it," Clint said, "but that's over. Now, I'm running toward it, not away from it."

"I wish you luck," Rex said, "and not just because, with you dead, I may lose a good job before I even start it."

"Don't worry," Clint said. "You'll have a job."

"Still," Rex said, "I *could* back your play." Rex took a shotgun from under the bar.

"No," Clint said, "I won't ask you to do that. Put it away."

Rex replaced the shotgun.

"But bring it with you to the new job," Clint said. "By the way, have you hired any bartenders?"

"I've talked to six men," Rex said. "I'm gonna choose two of them."

"That's good. How many girls do we have?"

"Three now, but I want at least five."

"Sounds good."

"I also thought we'd need some security," Rex said, "so I've talked to some other men about that."

"Seems like you have everything under control," Clint said. "I'm thinking I hired the right man to manage The Gunsmith Saloon."

"Thanks."

"But I have a question."

"What's that?"

"If we decide not to call it The Gunsmith Saloon," Clint said, "will you still want the job?"

"Definitely," Rex said. "It'll still be the biggest and best place in Laramie, no matter what you call it."

Chapter Forty-Four

Clint decided there was only one way to draw Holden out. He left The Union, walked into the street and stood in the center of it. Wagons and horses were forced to go around him.

People stopped on the boardwalks and stared at him.

"What's he doing?" somebody asked.

"Who knows?" someone else said. "He's just standing there."

"He looks like he's waitin'," another voice said.

The word got to Marshal Jackson, who left his office and walked over to join the crowd. There was no traffic on the street any longer, just Clint Adams standing there.

"What's goin' on, Marshal?" somebody asked.

"He's waitin'," Jackson said.

"For what?"

"Not what," Jackson said, "but who. He's waitin' for Ben Holden."

That information quickly spread through the crowd, and some of them started to move away, understanding what it meant. Others remained for an opportunity to see the Gunsmith in action.

***

Just as the word had gotten to Marshal Jackson, it found its way to Holden, who was in a small, off the main path saloon. At that time there was nobody there but a lazy bartender and the gunman. But another man came in, bellied up to the bar, and announced to the bartender, "The Gunsmith's standin' in the middle of Ivinson Avenue, waiting for Ben Holden."

The bartender shushed the man and pointed over to the table where Holden was sitting.

"Oh, shit," the man said. "Gimme a beer."

Holden stood up and carried his beer to the bar.

"Did you say he's waitin' for me?" he asked. "Or is he just standin' there?"

"Oh, well, he's just standin' there," the man replied, nervously.

"Then how do you know he's waitin' for me?"

"Well, uh, people was askin', and then the marshal came along and he said the Gunsmith was, uh, waitin' for you."

"Well," Holden said finishing his beer and slamming the empty mug down on the bar, "I guess I better not keep 'im waitin'."

"Hey, Holden," the bartender yelled as he went out, "why don't you settle your tab first?"

***

Clint saw Holden at the end of the street. At the same time the crowd on either side of the street saw him, too, and many of them thought better of standing there, and began to scatter. A lot of them ran into The Union, where Rex began selling them beers while they watched through the windows.

Holden began walking toward Clint, who stood his ground.

***

Somebody ran into the former Bucket of Blood and yelled to Stark and Spencer, "The Gunsmith's in the street with Ben Holden!"

"Jesus!" Stark yelled.

"Where?" Spencer asked.

"In front of The Union."

The man then ran out, so he wouldn't miss the action, and the two carpenters ran after him.

***

Holden stopped about ten feet from the Gunsmith and the two men stared at each other.

"It had to come to this, didn't it?" Holden asked.

"It didn't *have* to," Clint said, "but you forced it when you killed Bannister."

Holden laughed.

"That fat man threw his hammer at me," he said. "He was pretty quick with it, too. Almost took my head off before I put a bullet in his chest."

"So you're admitting that in front of all these people?" Clint asked.

"It don't matter," Holden said. "The marshal won't be able to do nothin' to me, and after I kill you, I'm leavin' town. Yeah, this place is gonna be too small for the man who killed the Gunsmith."

"Then there's nothing left to say," Clint told him.

"I guess not," Holden said, and drew.

He was fast. If Clint hadn't been an expert at seeing a man's move before he even made it, Holden might have outdrawn him. But Clint drew and plugged the man dead center. Holden's jaw fell just before his gun and he did.

Chapter Forty-Five

Two weeks later the new saloon was ready to open. Both Spencer and Stark had hired three more men each, so they could finish the job before Clint left town. He had given them two weeks.

As Clint came out of the hotel the morning of the opening, he found July Jackson standing on the porch.

"Now what?" Clint asked.

"Nothin' bad," Jackson said. "Just thought you'd like to know who stepped up and took the mayor's job."

"Not really," Clint said, since it really didn't matter to him, "but okay, who was it?"

"Nola Ketchum," Jackson said. "She's the only one who had the gumption."

"Well, good for her," Clint said. He pointed to the badge on Jackson's chest. "I see she's keeping you on as marshal."

"For the time being."

"Well, I guess the lady won't be at the opening to-night," Clint said.

"No, but the rest of the town council will be."

Clint stepped down from the porch, and that was when Jackson noticed his horse was there. Clint mounted Eclipse and looked at the lawman.

"Where are you off to?" Jackson asked.

"Leaving town."

"You're not going to the openin'?"

"Nope," Clint said.

"But . . . it's your place."

"It's Rick Hartman's place," Clint said. "I gave up my piece. It wasn't worth what I went through."

"Ain't you gonna say goodbye to anybody?"

"Already did, last night." In fact, Abby was still naked in his bed when he came down, and he had said a simple goodbye to Connie Rayland earlier. He had paid off the carpenters and turned the saloon over to Rex.

"I'm done with Laramie, for a while," Clint said. "Good luck to you, Marshal."

"And you," Jackson said.

Clint turned Eclipse and started riding down Ivinson Avenue. When he reached the saloon, he stopped briefly to look up at the sign. He had never been comfortable putting his moniker up there, over the door, and in the end Rick had understood. So he gave a short salute to HARTMAN'S SALOON AND GAMBLING HALL, and left town.

Coming May 27, 2020

THE GUNSMITH
459
The Imperial Crown

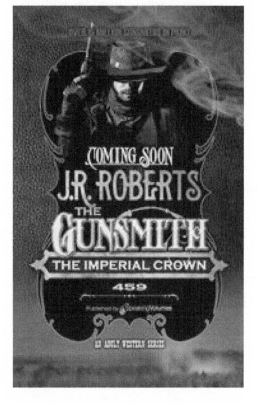

**For more information
visit:** www.SpeakingVolumes.us

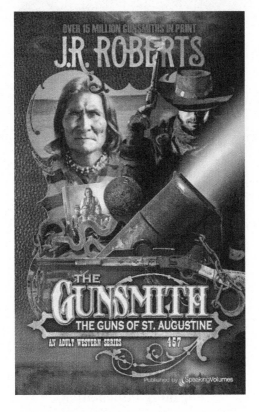

On Sale Now!

THE GUNSMITH *series*
Books 430 - 456

For more information
visit: www.SpeakingVolumes.us

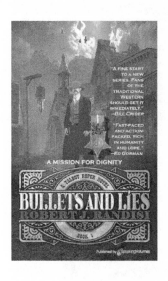 

On Sale Now!

Lady Gunsmith
Books 1 - 8
Roxy Doyle and the Silver Queen

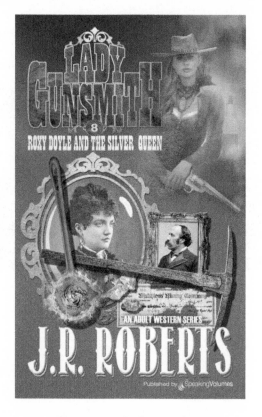

For more information
visit: www.SpeakingVolumes.us

On Sale!

Award-Winning Author
Robert J. Randisi (J.R. Roberts)

For more information
visit: www.SpeakingVolumes.us